ALFIE ~THE~ WEREWOLF

More books in the series

Birthday Surprise
Full Moon

Coming soon . . .

Wolf Wood
The Evil Triplets
Werewolf Secrets

ALFIE THE WEREWOLF

Silvertooth

Written by
Paul van Loon

Translated by
David Colmer

Illustrated by
Hugo van Look

Hodder
Children's
Books

A division of Hachette Children's Books

Copyright © 1996 Paul van Loon
Illustrations copyright © 1996 Hugo van Look
English language translation © 2010 David Colmer

First published in the Netherlands under the title *Silvertand*
by Uitgeverij Leopold in 1996

First published in Great Britain in 2010 by Hodder Children's Books
Published by arrangement with Rights People, London

The right of Paul van Loon and Hugo van Look to be identified as the
Author and Illustrator of the Work has been asserted by them in accordance
with the Copyright, Designs and Patents Act 1988

The publishers are grateful for the support of the Foundation
for the Production and Translation of Dutch Literature.

1

A Catalogue record for this book is available from the British Library

ISBN 978 0 340 98980 7

Typeset in Weiss by Avon DataSet Ltd,
Bidford on Avon, Warwickshire

Printed and bound in Great Britain by
CPI Bookmarque Ltd, Croydon, Surrey

The paper and board used in this paperback by Hodder Children's Books
are natural recyclable products made from wood grown in
sustainable forests. The manufacturing processes conform to the
environmental regulations of the country of origin.

Hodder Children's Books
a division of Hachette Children's Books
338 Euston Road, London NW1 3BH
An Hachette UK Company
www.hachette.co.uk

1

The Stranger

'*Wrow!* I never thought I'd ever be this happy. The first time I turned into a werewolf I was scared to death.' Alfie looked up at the stars. He had climbed on to the garden shed with Tim and now they were lying on their stomachs on the roof. It was almost November and leaves were drifting down into the garden.

From up on the roof they could see over the hedge and into the street that ran along the side of the house. Now and then people walked by without realizing that they were being spied on by a boy and a small white wolf wearing glasses.

'Look!' Tim whispered. 'That woman with the feather hat. She's just like Mrs Chalker. Do you remember her?'

'I sure do,' Alfie chuckled. 'I'm glad that nasty old bag is still locked up in the Reception Centre for Unusual People and Animals.'

Alfie gave a deep sigh and a quiet rumbling rose up in his hairy white throat. He looked up at the moon, which was almost full.

'*Wrow*, I live with a great family. You're almost a brother to me. Your mother is really sweet and your father is completely bonkers and sweet too. They know what I am and they don't care. This is the best family in the whole world.'

Tim smiled and scratched Alfie on the head. 'We think you're great too. You know that.'

Most of the time Alfie was an ordinary boy like Tim, but three times a month he was different, like now. That was when Alfie changed into a werewolf, a white werewolf with glasses. It happened at full moon, the night before full moon and the night after full moon. It was a big secret, of course, and almost no one knew about it.

'Hey, check *him* out!' Tim exclaimed.

Walking down the other side of the street was a big man dressed in a hat, boots and a long coat. He was smoking a cigar and trailing a wisp 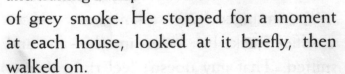 of grey smoke. He stopped for a moment at each house, looked at it briefly, then walked on.

'Strange guy,' Alfie said. 'He's looking for something.'

Tim nodded. 'Big and scary. Maybe he's a spy? Or someone from the mafia? What do you think, *pardner?*'

'Hit man,' said Alfie. 'Definitely. A cold-blooded killer. I wonder which one of our neighbours he's going to murder. Maybe the guy next door.'

The man strode on with big steps. Suddenly he crossed the road, coming closer and closer.

'Oops, he's walking this way,' Tim whispered.

Tim and Alfie lay perfectly still on the roof of the shed. The man stopped at the gate to their back garden. Smoke curled up out of his mouth like a long skinny ghost. The man peered round the garden inquisitively.

'Why doesn't he keep walking?' Alfie whispered. 'What's he looking in here for?'

Tim shrugged. 'Don't ask me.'

Alfie stuck his nose in the air and sniffed. 'That guy doesn't feel right to me. He smells funny.'

Suddenly the man turned his head towards the shed. Tim and Alfie flattened themselves against the roof. For a second there was a glint in his mouth. He threw the cigar on the ground, crushed it under his heel, then turned and disappeared in the shadows of the trees along the street.

'Who on earth was that?' Alfie asked.

Tim peered at the shadows. The man was nowhere to be seen.

'Just some stranger, I guess. He was probably lost.'

Alfie stretched his legs and wagged his tail.

'I have to go for a bit of a run.'

Tim nodded. 'Don't devour any chickens, Alfie. And make sure no one sees you! There are some funny people out and about, like that stranger.'

'*Wrow*, I can outrun any of them. And I bet we'll never see that guy again anyway.'

2

Uncle Seb

The doorbell rang early the next morning. It was Saturday and Tim and Alfie were still asleep.

Tim's father answered the door in bare feet. He was wearing his pyjamas – pink with yellow elephants – and still had curlers in his bright-blue hair. He'd dyed it the night before. He'd varnished his fingernails and toenails blue too. To go with his hair. Tim's father liked being different.

Still sleepy-eyed, he glanced through the frosted glass in the front door and saw a shadow on the other side. 'I don't know anyone that big,' he said, then opened the door.

It was a tall dark-eyed man with a long face. He was wearing a hat and a long coat and smoking a cigar. 'Good morning, I'm Uncle Seb. I've come for Alfie.' He blew a cloud of smoke into the hall.

Dad started coughing. 'Ugh-ugh! What do you mean, you've come for Alfie?'

The man smiled, with two dazzling front teeth glinting in the light. They were made of silver.

'I mean just what I said. From now on, *I'm* looking after Alfie. The judge has appointed me his guardian. I'm taking him with me.'

3

A Horrible Letter

Suddenly wide awake, Tim's father stared at the tall man. 'I'm sorry, but that's impossible. No, I mean, I'm not sorry at all. Alfie belongs here with us. We love him and we're keeping him.'

The man shrugged. 'Unfortunately for you, I have a court order right here. You're not his real family. I am.' He showed Dad a letter saying that Alfie had to go live with Uncle Seb.

'Who is it, William?' Tim's mother called from the living room.

9

Dad kept his eyes on the visitor. 'Someone called Uncle Seb. He's come for Alfie.'

'What!' Mum ran out into the hall. Like Dad, she was still in her pyjamas. Like Dad, she started to protest. 'That can't be true. It mustn't be. And what about school?'

'No problem. I'll take care of everything,' Uncle Seb said, blowing another cloud of cigar smoke into the hall.

'But . . . can't we do it tomorrow?' Mum asked. 'Or the day after tomorrow, or next year? Or when he's eighteen?'

Uncle Seb shook his head. 'No. Now!'

Tim came downstairs. He had heard everything. 'Alfie has to stay with us,' he shouted angrily and started to cry.

Then Alfie appeared on the stairs. He stood still for a moment, then sniffed. That's strange, he thought. That's the same smell as last night, that same funny smell!

'Listen, Alfie,' Tim's father said. 'There's something I have to tell you . . .'

Alfie turned pale when he heard the news. The lenses of his glasses misted over. 'I want to stay with Tim,' he stammered, but it didn't help.

'The judge has made his decision,' said Uncle Seb. 'From today, Alfie has to live with me.'

Tim's father read the letter at least ten times, but each time it said exactly the same thing and each time the official stamp from the court was just as impressive.

Everyone was sad. Everyone was miserable. Everyone was angry. But none of that was any help at all.

With a gloomy face, Alfie packed his suitcase in his bedroom. Tim helped.

'Did you recognize him, Alfie?'

Alfie took his glasses off for a moment to wipe his face with a hankie. Then he cleaned his glasses and put them back on. 'Who?'

'Uncle Seb,' Tim said. 'It's the man we saw last night.'

'I know. I smelt it coming down the stairs, that same funny smell.'

'What can we do?' asked Tim.

Alfie sniffed loudly. 'I'll make sure he can't wait to get rid of me. I'll make a racket and get into trouble. I'll make a mess of his house. I'll pee on his pot plants. I'll poo in his slippers. I bet you I'll be back home in two days!'

Alfie laid a photo of Tim and his parents in the suitcase. Tim handed him a pair of jeans.

'You have to be careful, Alfie. It's full moon tonight.' He tossed Alfie a jumper. 'That means you're going to turn into a werewolf again, just like last night. And again tomorrow. Uncle Seb mustn't find out.'

Alfie nodded. 'I'll be careful.'

'Alfie, what's keeping you?' Uncle Seb

called. 'We have to go. I've got a busy day ahead.'

Tim pressed a raggedy bear into Alfie's hands. 'Here, take my teddy. To remind you of me.'

Alfie's eyes filled with tears. 'I won't need reminding, I'll think about you the whole time! All of you! And I'll be back before you know it. You'll see.'

'And don't devour any chickens, Alfie.'

Alfie nodded. 'I promise!'

He looked around, wiped his nose and trudged downstairs with his case in one hand and Tim's bear under his arm.

Uncle Seb was still standing at the front door. Mum and Dad were in the living room comforting each other.

'Give me the suitcase,' said Uncle Seb. 'My car is a couple of streets away.'

'I don't want to go,' Alfie said quietly. 'Can't I just stay here?'

Uncle Seb screwed up one eye. His other eye bulged menacingly. He bent down to whisper in Alfie's ear. 'Listen, kid, don't make things difficult. The court has appointed me your guardian. If I have to, I'll call the police. Then your little buddy and his parents will be in trouble. Big trouble. Thanks to you, they might even end up in jail. You wouldn't want that to happen, would you?'

4

Gone

Alfie looked at the man in horror. Tim and his parents in jail?

Uncle Seb smiled and Alfie took a quick step back. He couldn't bear that smile. Now Uncle Seb winked, as if he hadn't just said something horrible and nasty.

Tim came downstairs. 'Is something wrong, Alfie?'

Uncle Seb gave a warning glare and Alfie shook his head. 'No, um . . . no. I'd better go now, I think.'

'That's very sensible of you,' said Uncle Seb.

Mum and Dad came out of the living room looking totally distraught.

'Bye, son. Give us a ring when you get there, OK?' said Mum. 'And have you got a warm coat with you?' She swallowed and looked away.

'I've written down Uncle Seb's address,' Dad said. '123 Donkey Street. We'll come and visit soon.' He pulled a hankie as big as a tea towel out of his pocket and honked into it.

'That's enough of that,' Uncle Seb said. 'We're going.' He picked up Alfie's suitcase and walked to the front door. 'It's better if you folks just stay here. That will be easier for everyone.'

Alfie quickly said his goodbyes. 'Bye, Tim. You're my best friend ever.' Then he ran off down the street after Uncle Seb before everyone could burst into tears again. I'll be back tomorrow or the day after anyway, he thought. I'll make sure of that. 'I'll call soon,' he shouted.

Tim, Mum and Dad stared at the closed door.

'Why on earth didn't we walk him to the car?' asked Dad.

Mum blew her nose in Dad's hankie. 'We should actually be glad for Alfie. Now he'll live with his real family. That's good, isn't it?'

'It's not good at all!' Tim shouted. 'That Uncle Seb can go and get lost for all I care.' His forehead puckered up with angry wrinkles. Then suddenly Tim looked happy. 'Now I get it! It's a dream. I must be asleep. That weird Uncle Seb doesn't even exist. If I pinch myself, I'll wake up and Alfie will be back.' He pinched his arm as hard as he could.

'Ow!' he screamed as a big red mark appeared on his arm.

It wasn't a dream. The whole house stank of Uncle Seb's cigar and Alfie was gone.

5

The Cage

Uncle Seb hurried down the street as if he couldn't wait to get away. Autumn leaves swirled around his feet. Alfie had to run to keep up.

Uncle Seb looked back over his shoulder. 'Come on, son, stop dawdling.'

'I'm doing my best.' Alfie hugged Tim's bear tight. 'Is the car very far away?'

Uncle Seb glanced back again, his dark eyes gleaming. 'We're almost there.'

They went around the corner and Uncle Seb pointed at a jeep.

'That's it.'

'Why is it all the way out here?' asked Alfie. 'Why didn't you just park in front of the house? Then Tim and Mum and Dad could have waved goodbye.'

'This was more convenient,' said Uncle Seb.

They had almost reached the Jeep, which had a trailer with a strange cage on it hooked up to the back.

Uncle Seb pulled a bunch of keys out of his coat pocket, opened the door and threw

Alfie's suitcase into the car. 'There.' Then he walked round to the cage. 'Look at this beautiful cage. It's got a door that slides up and locks with a padlock, see?'

Alfie nodded.

'Watch this,' said Uncle Seb, sticking a key into the padlock.

'What's the cage for?' Alfie thought it was a bit weird. 'Do you drive animals around sometimes? Do you work for the animal shelter or something?'

Uncle Seb slid the gate up, then turned. He grinned, showing two shining front teeth. 'This cage is for you!'

Uncle Seb grabbed Alfie, lifted him up and threw him into the cage. *Clang!* He'd locked it. Then he threw a big dark sheet over the top, blocking out the light.

Alfie heard a car door slam. The Jeep started up with a growl and the cage jolted into motion, knocking Alfie over. His head banged against the iron bars and everything went black.

6

Waiting

'Why hasn't Alfie called yet?' asked Tim. 'He's been gone for hours.'

He paced to and fro in front of the window, looking out into the street. He'd been doing it all day. Dad was sitting at the table. He had a map of the town spread out in front of him.

'Give Alfie a bit of time, Tim. He has to get used to his new house. He doesn't know where the telephone is or anything. And he has to unpack all his stuff . . .'

Dad bent over the map. He put on his

reading glasses and ran his finger down the list of streets. 'Where is Donkey Street anyway? I've never even heard of it.'

For the third time that day, Mum sprayed an entire can of pine-scented air freshener in the living room. The smell of Uncle Seb's cigar was very stubborn. She sighed deeply.

'I just hope Alfie has enough warm clothes with him. And what's going to happen tonight, when he turns into a wolf? We're used to it, but what will that Uncle Seb of his think?'

Tim stopped striding back and forth and lay down on the sofa. 'I wish he'd ring.'

Dad put on another pair of reading glasses. 'Strange,' he mumbled. 'Even with two pairs of reading glasses I can't find Donkey Street on this map.' He slid the map to one side. 'It must be somewhere in that new development.'

The doorbell rang and Mum, Dad and Tim all looked at each other, thinking and hoping the same thing.

Tim leapt up off the sofa, raced to the

front door and tore it open. The person standing there had a hat, a long coat and a walking stick.

'Hello, Tim,' said a growling voice. 'I get the feeling something very bad has happened!'

How...

7

All Alone

Alfie opened his eyes cautiously and rubbed his forehead. The bump on it throbbed painfully.

How did I get this bump? thought Alfie. And what time is it anyway? I wonder if Tim's up yet? I'd better go and wake him up.

He felt for the light switch, but couldn't find it. It was still pitch dark.

The next moment the floor he was lying on moved. Then Alfie remembered where he was: in a cage. Uncle Seb had locked him in and then covered the cage with a sheet. That

was why it was so dark and that was why
Alfie couldn't see where they were going.

Why did he do that? thought Alfie. What kind of weird uncle is he? First he wants me to come and live with him and then he locks me up as if I'm some kind of animal.

It's not fair! And I had to say goodbye to everyone in such a hurry.

Suddenly he thought of Noura. He hadn't even had a chance to say goodbye to her. That was terrible!

Noura was Alfie's girlfriend. She was in his class at school and she was special. She also knew his secret. When Alfie was near her, he always felt a warm glow inside.

When will I see her again? he thought. And Tim and his mother and his silly dad?

Alfie grabbed the bars of the cage and tried to shake them. They were made of iron: very hard and extremely strong.

He let go again with a sinking feeling in his stomach. It had all happened so fast. His eyes misted over, but he didn't want to cry. He hugged Tim's bear to his chest and stared into space. What's going to happen to me? he wondered.

A little later the car stopped suddenly, sending Alfie flying again. Fortunately he didn't bang his head on the bars this time. Alfie jumped up on to his feet. He still couldn't see any light anywhere.

'Uncle Seb,' he called, 'let me out.'

He heard the door of the Jeep open and close. Then footsteps and rustling leaves. The smell of a cigar drifted into the cage.

'Uncle Seb?'

No answer.

He heard some strange noises and, for a second, felt the cage move again.

'Uncle Seb, may I get out now?'

Feet shuffled through leaves. Someone coughed and cleared his throat.

Alfie grabbed the bars. 'Let me out!' he shouted.

The smell of the cigar grew stronger.

'Behave yourself, werewolf. It's not full moon yet!' Uncle Seb chuckled, sending a chill to Alfie's heart.

He knows! thought Alfie. Uncle Seb knows my secret. But how? Has someone betrayed me?

The footsteps moved away again.

'Uncle Seb,' Alfie called. 'Please let me out. Please, Uncle Seb, it's so dark in here. I'm scared.'

No answer came, only the slamming of the Jeep door. The car started and drove off, but the cage stayed motionless right where it was.

That's impossible, thought Alfie, but then he worked it out. Uncle Seb had unhooked the trailer and driven off.

He's left me behind, thought Alfie. All by myself.

Then he heard a sliding, scraping sound. And suddenly, close by, a high-pitched screech. It was the scream of a living creature and louder than the shriek of a dentist's drill.

Alfie felt a cold shiver run down his spine.

'Who's there?' he whispered.

8

Grandpa Werewolf

'Oh, it's you,' Tim said. 'Come in.'

He opened the door wider and the visitor stepped in, taking off his hat and hanging it on the coat rack. Yellow eyes stared at Tim from a black wolf's head.

It was Alfie's grandpa. He didn't need to wait until full moon to change into a wolf. He was one permanently. Long ago he had decided never again to take on human form. That was something that only very old werewolves, who had changed form many times, could do.

Grandpa Werewolf lived in the forest and came to visit some evenings. He was crazy about Alfie. Now he stared intently at Tim.

'So something *is* wrong,' he said. 'I can see it in your face. I smell it from your mood.' He strode into the living room. Mum and Dad didn't bat an eyelid.

Dad looked up from his map. 'Hello, Grandpa Werewolf.'

Grandpa growled and nodded hello. 'What's happened?'

'Alfie's gone,' Tim said in a quivery voice.

'What do you mean, gone? Has he run away? Did you have an argument?' The old werewolf's eyes flashed.

'No arguments,' Mum said. 'We never have any arguments with Alfie, you know that. He's the sweetest boy in the whole world.'

Tim nodded furiously. 'His uncle showed up.'

Grandpa Werewolf looked from Mum to Tim. 'His uncle? Which uncle? Where did he come from? What did he want?'

'Uncle Seb,' Mum said. 'He had a court

order. It said that from now on Alfie has to live with him.'

For a long time, Grandpa Werewolf didn't say a word. He sat down carefully on a chair and thought things through, holding his walking stick in his paws and leaning on it.

'Where is Alfie now?'

'He's gone with Uncle Seb,' Dad said. 'He had to. The judge had decided. There was nothing we could do.'

Grandpa Werewolf nodded, closing his eyes. When he spoke again, his voice was very soft. 'Listen, please think very carefully. What did this Uncle Seb look like? Did you notice anything unusual about him?'

Dad ran his fingers through his blue hair. 'He was big, that was the first thing I noticed.

And he wore a hat. That made it hard for me to get a good look at his face.'

'The cigar!' Mum said. 'He smoked a filthy cigar and stank out the whole house.'

Grandpa's wolf's head nodded gently. 'A cigar!' He still had his eyes shut, almost as if he was asleep. 'Was there anything else? Anything particularly unusual?'

'His teeth!' Tim said.

Slowly Grandpa opened his gleaming, deep-yellow eyes to study Tim. 'What about his teeth, Tim?'

'His two front teeth were both solid silver.'

Grandpa groaned and slumped slowly on his chair. His pointed ears drooped. His eyes turned a dull yellow. Suddenly he looked even older than he was. 'Silvertooth,' he mumbled. 'He's found Alfie!'

Mum moved closer with a worried expression.

'What did you say, Grandpa? Are you all right?'

Grandpa Werewolf sat up even more

slowly. His eyes spat fire. 'Sebarino Silvertooth, that's his name, the terror of all werewolves, and now he's got Alfie.'

9

Silvertooth

'Who's there?' Alfie asked again, his voice trembling. He held his breath and listened. The screeching sound had stopped. All he could hear now was a kind of snoring.

Alfie was covered in goosebumps. What kind of creature makes a noise like that? he wondered. He shook his head and sat down on the floor of the cage. He had no idea. All he knew was that the longer he sat there in the dark, the more frightened and lonely he felt.

Tim's bear was his only comfort. It smelt

like Tim and he pressed it against his cheek.

'Tim must be wondering why I haven't called,' he said to the bear. 'He might think I've already forgotten him. But I couldn't possibly forget him. Never! Even if I never see him again.'

Alfie was shocked by the very thought.

'Of course I'll see Tim again, bear. You wait, as soon as I get a chance I'm leaving. No way am I going to stay with Uncle Seb. As soon as I can, I'll break out of this cage. And then I'll go straight back to Tim's.'

The teddy bear looked at him silently with its beady black eyes.

Alfie sighed and wrapped his arms around his knees. What time was it? Maybe it was already dark. He was starting to get hungry and thoughts of tender chickens and bloody steaks rose up in him. That always happened at full moon.

Where's Uncle Seb gone? Is he coming back? Why has he left me behind like this?

Alfie scratched his head. He felt an itch, the werewolf itch! He grabbed the bars with both hands and tugged and jerked with all his might.

'Let me out!' he screamed, pulling as hard as he could. 'Let me out!'

The bars didn't give at all.

Suddenly he heard the sound of the Jeep. Uncle Seb was coming back. The engine turned off. A car door opened and closed. Footsteps.

Then the sheet slipped off Alfie's cage. It was still light, but the sun was already behind the trees.

'So, werewolf, I'm back again.'

Uncle Seb was standing in front of the cage, his Jeep parked a bit further away in front of a wooden shack.

'What are you calling me that for? My name is Alfie Span.'

Uncle Seb grinned. 'You think you can make a monkey out of me? I can smell a werewolf a mile away, so save your breath.' He folded up the sheet and carried it back to the Jeep.

Alfie looked around and saw trees, trees

everywhere. He was in a forest. There were other cages and pens around his, but he couldn't see what was in them.

One wooden box with just a small barred door at the front was shaking hard from side to side. Claws scratched on wood. Again Alfie heard the shrieking sound he had heard earlier.

Uncle Seb came back. He kicked the screeching creature's box. 'Shut up!'

It went quiet.

Uncle Seb turned around and looked at Alfie. Alfie peered back at him through the bars.

'Who are you really? You can't be a real uncle of mine. A real uncle wouldn't put me in a cage.'

Uncle Seb smiled. His silver teeth glinted in the last rays of sunlight. He was wearing silver rings on his fingers and a silver chain around his neck. There were shining silver buckles on his boots and his belt.

Alfie scuttled back to the rear of the cage. All that silver made him feel sick.

'I'll get some food for you, wolf. You need to be in good shape when the collectors come.'

Alfie's heart began to beat faster. 'Collectors? What do you mean?'

'You'll find out tonight,' growled Uncle Seb.

10

The Collectors

Tim and his parents looked at Grandpa in horror.

'What do you mean?' asked Mum. 'Do you think Alfie is in danger?'

Grandpa made a growling, groaning noise. His eyes were dark slits with a thin line of yellow.

'Sebarino Silvertooth has been infamous among us werewolves for a very long time. He has silver teeth and he wears silver jewellery. That protects him from all werewolves. We can't touch him. We're helpless against silver, you know that.'

'So he's not Alfie's uncle at all?'

Grandpa Werewolf growled. He picked up the letter and ripped it with his claw. 'Of course not. He's not anybody's uncle. Sebarino Silvertooth is a swindler and that court order is a fake. The court's stamp is a fake. Everything is fake because Silvertooth is a fake.'

'But why did he take Alfie away then?' asked Mum. 'What kind of person is he?'

Grandpa Werewolf closed his eyes. 'Silvertooth used to be a werewolf killer. He hunted werewolves and killed them. He hunted me once too, but I got away.'

Tim leapt up. 'Uncle Seb's a werewolf killer? Come on, we have to save Alfie. Now!'

Grandpa Werewolf opened his eyes again. 'Slow down, Tim. Silvertooth doesn't kill werewolves any more. Nowadays he's a businessman.'

'What kind of businessman?' asked Dad.

'A Dealer in Extraordinary Creatures.'

'A dealer in what?'

'Extraordinary Creatures: werewolves, extinct birds, strange species of animal and other unusual beings.'

'And what does he do with these Extraordinary Creatures?' Tim's voice was shaking.

'He sells them to collectors and researchers. Werewolves are worth a lot of money these days because there are so few of us left.'

For a moment Dad stared into space, dreaming. 'A collector of extinct creatures, that sounds like a very cool profession. Or a collector of creatures that don't actually exist, that's even cooler.'

A dig in the ribs brought him back to earth.

'Hey, Mr Cool,' Mum said, 'get back to the problem, will you? Alfie is in the hands of a fake uncle and you sit there dreaming about "cool" professions.'

Dad nodded, looking guilty. 'Um, sorry, stupid of me. What kind of person collects creatures, Grandpa?'

'An oddball, definitely. A weird, wealthy oddball dabbling in a strange hobby. The kind of person who keeps a private zoo at home.'

Tim imagined his friend in a cage in the home of someone who was weird, wealthy, odd and bald. Never! he thought.

'And what kind of researchers do you mean?' Dad asked.

Grandpa hesitated for a moment, looking at Tim. 'I'm afraid this won't be pleasant to hear. Silvertooth also sells his wares to researchers. They're usually people who want to know exactly how things are put together. They ask themselves questions like: Is there someone else under a werewolf's fur?'

'So what do they do?'

Tim didn't want to hear the answer.

'Researchers do experiments,' Grandpa said. 'They want to know what a werewolf looks like on the inside, so . . .'

The colour drained from Tim's face. 'They can't!' he cried. 'They're not allowed to cut Alfie open! Then I'll never see my friend again.'

11

The Pale Boy

Uncle Seb had gone away again. Fortunately, without replacing the sheet over Alfie's cage. The sun had set completely by now and the darkness was slowly emerging. There was no movement in the pens or the other cages. The strange, screeching creature seemed to have gone to sleep. Alfie could hear loud snoring coming from its box.

If only Tim was here, he thought. Tim's smart. He would be sure to come up with a plan of how to escape.

A pale moon crept out from behind the trees.

Alfie scratched himself on the head again. The werewolf itch was getting worse. He could smell strange smells and hear strange noises. His ears were already covered with thick white hair. Soon he would have changed completely and become a wolf. Suddenly he heard a noise from one of the pens.

'Oowah!'

Something was waking up and yawning.

'*Wrow!* Who's that?' asked Alfie, putting down Tim's bear. He already had a growly, werewolf voice.

He crept forward.

Something was moving in the cage next to his.

A thin face looked out through the bars. It was a pale boy with red lips and yellow spiky hair. He didn't look much older than Alfie.

'What you looking at me for?' he snapped, banging the bars with two clenched fists. 'Mind your own business, werewolf!'

Fierce eyes stared at Alfie. The boy snarled and spat like a wildcat. Sharp fangs gleamed in the corners of his mouth.

Alfie stepped back in fright. He curled up in the corner of the cage, pressing Tim's bear against his cheek. If only Tim was here! he thought again. Tim would protect me.

The boy banged on his bars again. He hissed and growled and snarled. 'Where you gone, wimp? What kind of werewolf are you? Say something if you dare!'

Alfie didn't answer. He didn't want to listen to the savage boy.

How does he know that I'm a werewolf? he thought. Is he a werewolf too? Or did he hear what Uncle Seb said? Either way he's vicious.

Alfie held on tight to the bear. I have to escape from here as fast as possible, he thought. I want to go back to Tim and his parents.

'Why don't you answer me?' the boy called. 'Why don't you say something?'

His voice sounded fainter and fainter and finally he stopped talking altogether. It was quiet for a while. Slowly it grew dark between the trees. A cloud slid in front of the moon.

Then Alfie heard soft sobbing. It was coming from the other cage, he was sure of it. The pale boy was crying softly to himself.

12

Track Tracer

'I've heard enough,' Dad cried, jumping up. 'We're going to go and get Alfie this minute. I've got Uncle Seb's address.'

He ran into the hall, grabbed his coat off the coat rack, slipped his feet into a pair of shoes and stumbled back into the living room.

He had the coat on inside out and he was wearing the shoes back to front.

'Well, what are you waiting for?' he asked.

Grandpa Werewolf looked at him

thoughtfully. 'So you know where Silvertooth lives, do you?'

Dad nodded. '123 Donkey Street. He gave me the address himself.'

Grandpa Werewolf scratched his head. 'I guess you looked on the map?'

Dad nodded.

'And I suppose Donkey Street wasn't on it?'

Again, Dad nodded. 'It must be in one of those new suburbs. That must be why it's not on the map yet.'

Grandpa shook his head forcefully. 'Just wake up! Donkey Street is not on the map because it doesn't exist. Sebarino Silvertooth wouldn't betray his hiding place! And there really is no chance of Alfie calling. This is a very serious situation, people. Alfie has been kidnapped by the smartest and most dangerous werewolf hunter of all. And we don't know where he is.'

Dad, Mum and Tim looked at each other.

'But . . . how are we going to find him then?' Tim's lower lip was trembling. 'Where should we look for him, Grandpa? Or . . . will we never see Alfie again?'

Grandpa Werewolf sighed. 'I don't know, son. There's only one way for us to find him. We need a track tracer.'

'A what?' Mum asked.

'A track tracer. Someone who can follow Alfie's track from here. Someone with a highly developed sense of smell. A werewolf, in other words. But where can I find one?'

They looked at Grandpa.

'Grandpa, you're a werewolf yourself, aren't you?' Mum said gently. 'Or had you forgotten?'

Grandpa shook his head. 'Of course not. I'm not mad, you know. I'm just too old. My sense of smell is nowhere near as good as it used to be. All the smells outside would just confuse me.'

'And a tracker dog?' asked Tim.

'Preferably not, son. Dogs can only follow a track on the ground. Werewolves can sniff out the slightest trace of a track on the ground or in the air from miles away. That's why we need a young, energetic werewolf.'

He leant heavily on his walking stick and closed his eyes for a moment. Then he suddenly raised his head. 'Leo! We need Leo. He's always in the forest somewhere. I have to go and look for him.'

Mum, Dad and Tim remembered Leo. He was a cousin of Alfie's and a werewolf too. A fairly fierce one actually, but he was fine once you got to know him.

Grandpa clambered up on to his feet. 'I'm off. As soon as I've found Leo, we'll come here. Maybe tonight. Maybe not until tomorrow night.'

'Tomorrow night!' cried Tim. 'Will we have to wait that long before we start looking? What if Alfie gets sold to weird researchers or collectors tonight?'

Grandpa Werewolf put his hat on with a mournful look in his eyes. 'I really am doing my very best, Tim, but first I have to find Leo.'

Tim nodded. 'I know, Grandpa. Sorry.'

Grandpa growled a goodbye and hurried

off. Dad stared at the closed door.

'So all we can do is wait,' he said. 'Sh—'

'William! There's no need to start using language like that,' Mum said.

'Sorry,' Dad said 'I just wish we knew another werewolf. Then we could start track tracing straightaway.'

A couple of hours later the front doorbell rang. Tim leapt up and went to get it. 'That's fast. Grandpa must have found Leo already.'

He opened the door to find a girl with long black hair standing there smiling at him. She had brown eyes with golden flecks in them.

'Noura!' Tim said.

'Hi, Tim, is Alfie home?'

13

Valentine

The boy in the other cage sobbed softly.

Alfie stood up and walked to the front of his cage. Complete darkness had descended over the forest, but suddenly the moon was shining like a white lamp. Alfie felt the wonderful feeling of its light on his skin. His cheeks were already covered with white hair, and white fur was growing on his hands too. He pressed his face up against the bars.

'Hey, pssst! What's wrong? Why are you crying?'

The boy was sitting hunched up near his bars. He peered over his shoulder at Alfie and quickly wiped his eyes. His eyebrows turned into an angry stripe.

'I'm not crying at all. Why don't you mind your own business anyway, busybody!'

'I'm sorry,' said Alfie. 'I was just trying to be friendly.'

'Tssss! Friendly! What use is friendly? Where's it going to get you? I don't want anything to do with your kind.'

'My kind? What do you mean? Aren't you a werewolf too?'

Immediately the boy hissed like a wildcat. He gripped the bars so tightly his knuckles turned white. 'A werewolf? Me? You can't be serious! What do you take me for?' He spat at the ground through the bars, then suddenly bared his teeth. They were pearly white and perfectly straight. His eye-teeth were long and sharp.

'I am Valentine. I am a vampire. Vampires are much nobler creatures than werewolves. We live for ever.'

Alfie looked at the boy with astonishment.

'A vampire? Yeah, right. Everyone knows vampires don't exist.'

A fierce look appeared in Valentine's eyes. 'Really? And what about werewolves? Or do you believe you don't exist either?'

Alfie blushed under his white hair. That was pretty stupid of him. 'So . . . you drink blood?' he said. 'That's what vampires do, isn't it?'

Valentine nodded. 'A refined beverage for refined creatures. But that's beyond the comprehension of brutes like you who prefer to rip everyone to shreds.'

Alfie was shocked. 'I . . . I'm not a brute. And I never rip anyone to shreds. I've never done anything like that. Well, except maybe a chicken or two, by accident.'

Tears leapt to his eyes, but Valentine just gave a mocking laugh.

'Of course not. Of course you haven't. You werewolves are all the same. I don't like werewolves. And I especially don't like werewolves with funny glasses. Tssss!'

Suddenly the terrible screeching started up again.

It was coming from the box next to Valentine's cage. The box juddered up and down with a sound of rattling iron. For a second a thin tail whipped out through the bars.

'Who's in that cage?' whispered Alfie. 'What kind of creature makes a noise like that?'

'A Scoffle!' replied Valentine.

'A scuffle?'

'Wow, you don't know anything, do you? A Scoffle, I said. An extremely dangerous creature. As small as a cat, but able to strip an elephant down to its bones in two minutes flat. Fortunately it sleeps most of the time. Then it snores like a bear.'

The box shuddered even harder. The wood creaked. The chain rattled. It seemed like the Scoffle was going to break free any minute.

Alfie hugged Tim's bear tighter. Valentine

laughed scornfully.

'Look at that, a werewolf with a teddy bear. You're not a werewolf, you're a werewimp!'

Suddenly light swept over the trees and shone on the cages. Valentine hunched over and groaned. He wrapped his arms around his body. All at once he too was a scared little boy.

'Oh, Silvertooth is coming back,' he moaned. 'What's he going to do with me?'

14

Noura

'What? Alfie's living at his uncle's from now on?'

Noura was sitting on the sofa next to Tim, who had told her everything. Completely stunned, she looked at Tim and his parents.

'Won't we ever see him again? That's not right.'

'No,' Tim said, 'it's not. That uncle isn't even a real uncle. We found that out from Grandpa Were . . . Oops.'

Tim quickly swallowed his words. He wasn't allowed to say anything about werewolves, of course. No one knew Alfie's secret.

'Oh, you mean Grandpa Werewolf?' said Noura.

Staggered, the others looked at her. Noura smiled and scratched her head.

'I know all about it, you know. Alfie told me that his grandfather is a werewolf.'

Dad ran his fingers through his blue hair and looked at Mum. She shrugged. 'And didn't you find that a little strange, Noura?'

The girl shook her head. 'No. What's strange about it? Alfie's a werewolf himself, after all.'

Tim and his parents' mouths dropped even further.

'So you know!' Tim exclaimed. 'Alfie could have told us.'

Noura scratched her neck. 'Maybe he forgot to mention it. But what happens now?'

'We want to go looking for Alfie,' said Dad. 'We're waiting for Grandpa Werewolf. He's gone looking for a track tracer.'

'A what?'

'A track tracer. That's someone who can sniff out Alfie's track. Only a werewolf has a sense of smell that's good enough.'

Tim nodded. 'But Grandpa Werewolf is too old.'

Noura used both hands to scratch her head. 'When will Grandpa Werewolf be here then?'

Tim sighed. 'Maybe soon. But maybe not until tomorrow evening.'

Noura stood up and scratched her neck hard. She now seemed to be itchy all over. 'We can't wait that long. Shall we start searching now. I'll help.'

Mum smiled. 'That's very sweet of you, dear, but without a track tracer we'll never find him.'

Noura looked at Mum. Suddenly her eyes turned darker. 'I'll be the track tracer.'

15

Feeding Time

The Jeep pulled up next to the wooden shack. Uncle Seb got out and strode over to the cages. He was holding a whip in one hand and carrying a big bag in the other. He cracked the whip.

'Feeding time!' he shouted, putting the bag down next to Valentine's cage. 'And I've got some good news, boys. I've got buyers. They're coming tonight.'

He reached into the bag and pulled out a bottle of something red. 'Here, vampire, drink up. You have to look healthy later because a collector wants to buy you. Mr O'Navlon collects anything to do with vampires: books, films, dolls, paintings. But he hasn't got a real vampire yet. He wants to get you stuffed and mounted. Nice, huh?'

Valentine was sitting at the back of his cage. He had his head hidden between his knees and didn't look up.

Uncle Seb slid the bottle in through the bars. 'Drink up, bloodsucker. It'll put a blush on those pale cheeks of yours. That will look cute when you're stuffed.' He turned around. 'I've got a delicious little snack for you too, werewolf cub.' He slid the whip in behind his silver belt buckle. 'And a buyer too, most likely. No one less than Dr Cutter himself. He loves werewolves and he loves his research.'

'Research?' The word scared Alfie. 'What kind of research? I don't want any research. I want to go home to Tim.'

But Uncle Seb didn't answer. He opened the bag again and a frightened cackling came out of it. 'Look what we've got here, a hensome chicken. Sink your teeth into this, werewolf. Dr Cutter likes his werewolves plump and tender. They're easier to dissect.'

Uncle Seb held the chicken up by its legs. It flapped and beat its wings. Feathers floated through the air as he rattled his keyring. 'Get back, werewolf. I'm going to open your cage for a moment.'

He brought his face up to the bars and bared his silver teeth. Alfie cringed back. The silver weakened him and made him feel sick. The padlock creaked.

Uncle Seb slid the door up and pushed the chicken into the cage. It immediately started running round and round in terrified circles.

Suddenly the Scoffle let out a

blaring, ear-piercing screech. Uncle Seb slammed the sliding door and spun around, pulling out his whip and cracking it.

'Shut up, you horrible creature. They can hear you out on the motorway. That screeching of yours is going to betray my hideaway. I've warned you, now I have to teach you a lesson.'

He walked over to the Scoffle's box and kicked it. Then he poked the whip in through the bars. The Scoffle screeched even louder. A bloodcurdling cry of rage. Suddenly its skinny tail shot out through the bars and wrapped around Uncle Seb's leg. Uncle Seb bashed the tail with his whip.

'Off, you cheeky monster!'

The Scoffle screeched, pulled its tail back in and fell silent. Uncle Seb wiped the sweat off his forehead and rolled up the whip.

'So, that's that taken care of. That thing has to know who's boss around here. And so do you! I'm going to have dinner and then take a nap. The buyers will be here in a couple of hours, so behave.'

He strode off towards the wooden shack.

Alfie sat motionless in his cage, where the frightened chicken was still fluttering around and banging its wings against the bars. Alfie didn't even look at it. Every hair on his body was motionless. He stared at the wooden shack out of the corner of his eye, hoping that Uncle Seb wouldn't stop or turn around.

Uncle Seb went in and pulled the door shut behind him. A light flicked on inside the shack.

'*Wrow!*' growled Alfie quietly, his heart pounding with excitement.

Uncle Seb had forgotten something.

Alfie's cage looked as if it was shut, but Uncle Seb hadn't locked it. Because of the Scoffle's screeching, he'd forgotten all about the padlock.

All I have to do, thought Alfie, is slide up the door.

16

Not Fair

Black hair started growing on Noura's face. Her ears turned pointy and her hands changed to paws. Her nose stretched and transformed into a snout.

Tim gasped with surprise. 'Noura, you're a werewolf too! So that was why you were scratching so much. You had werewolf itch.'

For a second Tim and his parents looked like statues with gaping mouths.

'I can't believe it,' Dad said at last. 'You too, Noura? You too? Everyone else turns into a werewolf just like that. And not me. That's not fair.'

Noura grinned. 'But it is useful. Now I can be the track tracer.'

Her voice had a funny little growl to it. Tim was so excited he couldn't talk properly.

'Noura, how come you're . . . I mean . . . Why? When? What happened? Who?'

Noura gave a friendly growl. 'Because of Alfie of course. He bit me by accident during the school trip. At full moon. I found out the next night when I suddenly got all hairy. Before I knew it, I was walking around on all fours.'

Tim nodded. 'So Alfie already knows?'

'Yes, of course. And Grandpa Werewolf knew too. Even before I did.'

'Wasn't it a terrible shock?' asked Mum. 'Weren't you horrified?'

Noura shook her head. 'I thought it was fantastic. I came straight over to see Alfie so we could howl at the full moon together. It's so much fun!'

Dad sighed deeply. 'I'd like to do that too, howling at the full moon. Fantastic.'

Mum glanced at him lovingly. 'We know that, William. But right now we don't have any time to waste.'

Noura nodded. 'That's right, we have to look for Alfie. And find out whether I'm a good track tracer.' She hesitated. 'Um, you'll have to drive. We don't know how far it is and I'm a very fast runner. Ordinary people can never keep up with us.'

Dad groaned. 'Bah, ordinary people. I don't want to be ordinary. Ohhh, if only I was different.'

'Stop moaning, William,' Mum said. 'I like you just the way you are. You act weird enough as it is. Now put on a coat and get the car.'

A little later Tim and his parents were sitting in the car. Dad had a green diving mask on his forehead and an upside-down flowerpot on his head. He was wearing an old fur coat with an enormous collar that had belonged to Mum.

Noura sniffed around the garden.

'Do you think she'll find Alfie's track?' Tim asked.

'I'm sure she will,' said Mum.

Suddenly Noura froze. She pressed her nose against the ground, then stuck her head up in the air and sniffed. She stretched her neck and howled at the moon. 'Woohooo!'

That was the signal. Noura had found the track.

Her wolf's howl went up once more and then she shot out of the garden like a rocket.

'Go!' Tim shouted. 'She's found Alfie's track! We mustn't lose her. Soon I'll see my friend again.'

Dad slid the diving mask down in front of his eyes and pushed the accelerator flat to the floor. 'Passengers, hold on, it's time for take-off!'

17

Werewolf Hunger

'Shhh, be quiet,' Alfie growled at the chicken.

He sighed and sat down on the floor. The chicken was still cackling with terror. Alfie's stomach rumbled. The werewolf hunger was enormous. He ran his tongue over his teeth.

'No way,' Alfie growled to himself. 'I don't eat chickens any more. I promised Tim.'

The chicken was running round the cage in frightened circles.

'Calm down,' Alfie whispered. 'I won't hurt you. Really, I won't. But you have to be quiet, otherwise Uncle Seb will come back.'

The chicken wasn't listening. Either that or it didn't understand Werewolf. It cackled and beat its wings against the bars. Feathers floated through the cage.

Alfie leapt up. 'That's enough!' He curled his claws. He bared his teeth. Then he gave one very loud growl. *'WROW!'*

The chicken shut up at once. It fell over backwards and lay there motionless in a corner of the cage as if it was frozen, with its feet in the air, its beak closed and its wings spread. It watched Alfie with big frightened eyes.

'Good,' he growled. 'I'm sorry, but at least you're quiet now.'

He looked at Uncle Seb's shack. Fortunately no one had come out.

There was no movement in Valentine's cage either. Maybe he was asleep.

All the better, thought Alfie. He's not nice anyway.

Alfie reached out to the padlock. He hardly dared believe it, but it really was open. How lucky can you get?

He unhooked the lock and threw it away, then slid up the door.

The chicken was still as quiet as a mouse.

Alfie looked left and then right. Moonlight shone on the trees. A small light was on in Uncle Seb's shack. Uncle Seb didn't come out.

Carefully Alfie stepped out of the cage.

Saved! he thought, spreading his claws, stretching and wagging his tail. 'Freeeee!' And now back home to Tim.

He felt like howling at the moon at the top of his lungs, then getting out of there as fast as he could.

There was still no sound from Valentine's cage. The Scoffle was snoring loudly. It was the perfect moment to escape.

No one could see him. No one could hear him.

Then he remembered something important just in time. Tim's bear was still in the cage. He'd almost forgotten it. He rushed back into the cage to grab it.

And now he had to get away fast.

He glanced at Valentine's cage.

No, he thought, I can't leave like this. I have to help Valentine escape. After all, he's a bit like me: not a monster, but not an ordinary kid either. Even if he's as friendly as a rattlesnake with a sore throat.

Alfie wavered, hopping from one foot to the other.

How am I going to get his cage open without a key? he wondered. Can I break it open? Or bite through the bars?

'Where do you think you're sneaking off to?' Valentine's pale face appeared in the moonlight. In one hand he was holding the bottle Uncle Seb had put in his cage. There wasn't a drop of blood left in it. Valentine wiped his mouth. 'So you wanted to escape, did you, leaving me behind? Think again, werewolf!' The vampire laughed. 'I think I'll just call Silvertooth. He'll be very grateful. Maybe he'll even let me go.'

Alfie was so shocked he didn't know what to do. 'No, Valentine, don't, I was trying, I wanted . . .'

But Valentine had already started shouting. 'SILVERTOOTH! THE WEREWOLF IS OUT!' He smashed the bottle against the bars, sending glass tinkling to the ground. In the same instant the Scoffle started screeching, the petrified chicken started cackling again and the shack door flew open.

Uncle Seb stormed out in his pyjamas, hair wild and gun at the ready.

18

Red Light

Tim's father swung the steering wheel. The green diving mask and the flowerpot made him look very unusual, a bit like an alien pilot.

'Faster, William,' said Mum. 'Noura's not wasting any time. Where is she now?'

'There she is,' Tim shouted. 'On that road on the other side of the field.'

Like a black shadow, Noura ran on in the moonlight, stopping now and then to stick her nose in the air and sniff, then running on again.

Dad jerked the steering wheel.

'What are you doing?' Mum cried.

'I'm taking a short cut, otherwise we'll lose her.' Dad raced up on to the pavement, sideswiping a planter box and destroying a rubbish bin.

'Watch out for the lamppost!' screamed Tim.

Crack! The right wing mirror snapped off.

Another tug on the wheel and they were driving over the field. Mum and Tim bounced on their seats. The field was rough and very bumpy.

'There she goes!' shouted Tim. 'Ow!'

His head banged on the roof of the car. So did Mum's.

'Glad I'm wearing a flowerpot,' Dad mumbled.

He pulled on the steering wheel again and tore right across the field. Soon he was on the road on the other side.

Noura was a distant dot running down the middle of the road. Cars beeped furiously, but Noura ignored them. She reached a crossroads with traffic lights and ran straight through the amber light without stopping. Angry drivers wound down their windows to shout at her. 'Stupid dog. Where's its owner?'

'Faster, Dad,' Tim cried. 'It's almost red.'

Dad had his foot to the floor, but the traffic light turned red. There was a police car on the other side of the intersection and Dad had no choice but to slam on the brakes.

'Drat!' He wiped the glass of his diving mask clean. In the distance Noura kept running.

'Hurry up, hurry up,' Tim mumbled. 'Change to green, why don't you?' He wrung his hands and drummed his feet. The light was still red. Slowly the police car came driving up from the other side of the intersection and stopped next to Dad's car. The policeman wound down his window, gesturing for Dad to do the same.

'You have a flowerpot on your head,' the policeman said. 'Did you know that?'

The light turned green, but the policeman wouldn't drive on.

'Of course I know that,' Dad said, raising his diving mask. 'Sometimes I wear a tea cosy, sometimes it's a flowerpot. That's not against the law, is it?'

The policeman shook his head. 'No, but it is a bit potty!' He smiled and waited for a moment. 'A bit potty . . . get it?'

But Dad didn't laugh. 'May I drive on now, officer? I don't have time for corny jokes. We're running late as it is.'

Behind them cars started to beep.

'OK, drive on,' the policeman said gruffly.

'But not as fast as you just drove up. I saw that, buddy. Don't forget.'

Dad nodded, wound up the window and tore off.

'William, he said not so fast.'

'I was doing fifty-five a minute ago,' Dad replied. 'Now it's just over fifty, so I'm doing what he said.'

They drove on until they came to a T-junction where they could turn right or left.

'Oh, no!' Dad pulled over to the side of the road.

'What are you doing, William?' Mum asked.

Dad shook his head. 'I don't know which way Noura went. We've lost her!'

19
Traitor

'Don't move, werewolf. I've got silver bullets in this gun. They're fatal for werewolves, so they can definitely kill a werewolf cub!'

The Scoffle gave a shrill shriek, but Uncle Seb ignored it. Slowly he walked up to Alfie. 'Back into your cage, wolf, or I'll shoot a hole right through you.'

Alfie's ears lay flat against his head. He took slow backward steps. Valentine pressed his face against the bars and sniggered.

'You traitor,' whispered Alfie. 'What did

you do that for? I was going to help you escape too.'

'Yeah, sure!' hissed Valentine. 'A werewolf who helps a vampire? That'll be the day. But it's not your day today, chump. You've had it now, but I'll be free, you'll see. Silvertooth will be very grateful.'

Alfie shook his head. 'I don't think so.'

Uncle Seb came closer. He pointed at the cage with his gun. 'Go on, into your cage, wolf. And no more funny stuff.'

Alfie looked around quickly.

Maybe, he thought, if I run really fast.

Uncle Seb grinned, moonlight splashing on his silver teeth. 'I wouldn't try it, wolf. You're fast, but my bullets are faster. Within three seconds you'd be a sieve. And that would be a shame because Dr Cutter prefers his werewolves undamaged, without any holes in them. He likes to make his own holes.'

Uncle Seb sniggered.

Alfie hung his head.

Then he growled and leapt at Uncle Seb,

taking him by surprise. He was as fast as lightning, his claws flashing in the moonlight. Uncle Seb dropped his gun in fright, but Alfie bumped into something. It was as if Uncle Seb was surrounded by an invisible wall. Dazed, Alfie fell to the ground.

Uncle Seb looked at him and smiled, then opened his coat to reveal silver necklaces, silver belts and silver buttons. 'You little twerp. Do you think you can resist this? There's not a werewolf born that can touch me. I'm protected by silver. Now, get into your cage!'

Defeated, Alfie crawled back into the cage. The chicken fluttered out quickly and ran off cackling.

Uncle Seb closed the door, this time locking it. 'Too bad about the chicken, wolf. You'll just have to go to bed without any supper.' He sniggered again.

Alfie growled. Inside he was furious at himself. And he was furious with Valentine, the traitor. Why was I so stupid? he thought. Why did I want to free him too? He's not worth it. He's just a good-for-nothing vampire.

Valentine coughed. 'Um, Mr Silvertooth?' His voice was as sweet as honey.

Uncle Seb turned around. 'What do you want, bloodsucker?'

Valentine rubbed his pale hands together nervously. 'Well, I thought . . . I thought, seeing as I warned you . . . about the werewolf escaping and that . . . I thought maybe you might want to let me go . . . Now, I mean . . . OK?'

Uncle Seb scratched his head. 'So you thought that, did you? Oh, hmm, I'll have to think about it. Maybe you're right. You did do me a favour.' He lay a finger against his nose thoughtfully.

Two seconds later he looked at Valentine. 'No, I don't think so. I'd rather keep you here. The collectors will be arriving soon. I mustn't disappoint them.'

Valentine's face turned pale green. 'But I helped you. Otherwise you'd have lost the werewolf.'

Uncle Seb smiled. It was a vicious smile full of malice and gleaming silver. 'You're absolutely right. Thanks for your help.' Then Uncle Seb walked back to his shack.

Valentine stuck his arms out through the bars, clawing the air with his fingers. 'I want to get out of here! I don't want to be stuffed! I'm only 200 years young. I have a whole undead life in front of me.' He burst into tears.

Uncle Seb just went into his shack without a backward glance.

Alfie sat motionless in his cage. Valentine had betrayed him. Valentine was a nasty vampire who had made fun of him and called him a werewimp. But Alfie still felt sorry for him.

'Don't cry, Valentine,' Alfie growled. 'We have to think this through. There must be a way to escape.'

Valentine wiped away his tears. 'Escape? How? We don't have any keys. We'll never get out of here.'

'My friend Tim will think of something,' said Alfie.

'Wow, have you got a friend?' Valentine asked. 'I wish I did. I don't think I've ever had a friend. Everyone's too scared I'll bite them. Life's not fair.'

Once again tears appeared in Valentine's eyes. He crawled off into the darkest corner of his cage and sat there sniffling.

Alfie didn't pay him any more attention. Tim is really smart, he thought. He'll be sure to come looking for me. He knows I would have phoned home, but I haven't. He'll definitely be worried. Maybe . . .

But suddenly Alfie hung his head. Tim doesn't have a clue where I am. Nobody does. I don't even know myself. And I'm not smart enough to think up a good plan. I'm just a stupid werewimp.

He sat down despondently and peered for a long time at the bushes around the cages.

Was that something moving?

No, it can't be, thought Alfie, but for a moment there . . .

He rubbed his eyes with his white forepaws and wiped his tears away. Then he looked again.

It was true. Something was moving in the bushes. There was someone there.

20

What Now?

Tim and his parents sat in the car feeling miserable. Noura was nowhere in sight. Dad scratched his head under his flowerpot. He pushed the diving mask up to his forehead.

'What now? Noura forgot all about us, of course. She's tracking Alfie and that's all she thought about. Werewolves are like that. They follow their instinct and forget the rest.' Dad sighed. 'It must be amazing!'

Tim bounced up and down impatiently on the back seat. 'We can't just sit here dreaming, Dad. If we drive fast we might catch up with Noura.'

Mum shook her head. 'But if we head in the wrong direction we'll lose her completely. We're better off waiting. Maybe Noura will retrace her steps when she finds out she's lost us.'

Dad sighed again. 'What am I supposed to do now? I don't know what to do.'

'I do,' Mum blurted. 'I'm going to call Noura's parents. Give me your mobile, William.'

Surprised, Dad gave Mum his mobile phone. 'Do you think Noura's parents know where she is now?'

Mum shook her head as she typed in the number. 'Of course not, silly. That's the point. They don't know where Noura is.' She held the phone up to her cheek. 'Hi, this is Alfie's mother . . . Yes, that's right. Noura is here at our house, that's what I'm calling about. They're having such fun together. Is it all right with you if Noura stays over tonight? . . . Yes, of course, we'd love to have her. OK, then . . . Yes, bye.'

Mum handed the phone back with a sigh. 'There. That was a bit of a fib, but it was for their own good. Now *they* at least won't be worried. All we have to do is get Noura and Alfie back and then everything will be fine.'

Tim didn't answer. When his mother put it like that it sounded simple. But what if they never saw Alfie again? It was a terrible thought and Tim quickly put it out of his mind.

He pressed his nose up against the window and saw two figures running down the middle of the road in the darkness. One was wearing a big cap and the other had a hat on, and the two figures were roped together.

They were definitely no ordinary joggers. The front one made strange, gigantic leaps, stopping now and then to sniff the air, then running on. The one at the back obviously found it hard to keep up and was almost being dragged along behind the other one.

Tim's eyes widened and he started panting with excitement. The window steamed up immediately and he couldn't see a thing. Quickly he wiped the glass clean. The two figures were close now. Tim leapt with joy, banging his head on the roof of the car again.

'Tim, what's got into you?' Mum said. 'You're acting as weird as your dad.'

But Tim was beside himself. 'Look, Mum, Dad! There! Grandpa Werewolf and Leo!'

21

Saved!

Alfie saw brown eyes with golden speckles.
Pointy black ears and a black wolf's muzzle.
He almost leapt with excitement. A small
black werewolf was sitting in the bushes,
with just her head sticking up over the leaves.
She stuck her snout in the air, looked left,
looked right and then looked straight ahead
at Alfie's cage.

Alfie could hardly believe it. Noura was
sitting over there in the bushes, less than
twenty metres away from him. How did she
get there? Or was it someone else?

Again he rubbed his eyes with his forepaws. When he looked back, Noura was still there. She waved.

I'm saved, thought Alfie. Noura has come to rescue me. But he didn't dare call out. He glanced over at Uncle Seb's shack. It was dark and there was no movement. Suddenly his joy turned to fear.

Wait a second, he thought. Noura can't free me. She doesn't have a key. Her being here is actually horribly dangerous. Uncle Seb mustn't see her, otherwise he'll lock her up too.

Alfie gestured with a paw, 'Go away, run away.'

But Noura didn't understand and waved back cheerfully.

'Oh, no,' Alfie groaned softly. 'Go away now, please, Noura.'

'Who are you talking to, werewolf?' Valentine's pale face appeared behind his bars. 'What's going on?'

Alfie just pointed.

Valentine squinted and peered. 'What's that I see? Another werewolf?'

Alfie nodded. 'That's Noura, my girlfriend.'

'Wow!' said Valentine in a jealous voice. 'You've got a girlfriend too?' He sounded like he might start crying again. 'And I don't have anyone at all. Nobody likes me.'

I'm not surprised, thought Alfie, but it was still sad, someone not having a single friend.

'Please don't betray her, Valentine. Otherwise Silvertooth will catch her too.'

The vampire nodded. 'Don't worry. I won't

say a word to Silvertooth. I'll be as quiet as a bat. Even if I don't think it's fair that you have a girlfriend and I don't.'

Silently they stared at Noura.

'What's she doing here?' whispered Valentine.

Alfie looked back at Silvertooth's shack, where the windows were still dark. Noura crept closer, hiding behind the next bush.

'I think she wants to set me free.'

Valentine sighed. 'Oh, that must be so fantastic. So ultra-romantic. A girlfriend risking her life to rescue you.'

Alfie gritted his teeth. 'It's not fantastic at all. It's just stupid. It's way too dangerous here. If Silvertooth catches her, he'll stick her in a cage too. I have to chase her off.'

Cautiously Noura emerged from the bushes.

'What can I do?' Alfie groaned. 'How do I get her out of here in a hurry?'

'Easy enough,' whispered Valentine. 'Call her names. Be mean. That's what I always do. It gets rid of anyone.'

'You sure?' Alfie asked.

Valentine nodded. 'Be mean and nasty to her, she'll be gone in no time.'

Alfie hesitated. He didn't like to be mean to people, but he had no time to come up with another plan.

On all fours, Noura crept over to Alfie's cage. 'Hi, Alfie.' She stood up and laid her forepaws between the bars. 'I'm so glad I've found you.'

'I'm not,' growled Alfie. 'Go away, Noura.'

22

Grandpa and Leo

Tim and his parents leapt out of the car.

'Grandpa Werewolf!' Tim called.

The figure with the hat looked at him with surprise. The other one was a big fellow, dressed in a cap and a long raincoat. His paws were covered in mud and the tip of a tail was sticking out from under his coat. He had a wolf's muzzle, just like Grandpa.

'Tim?' Grandpa Werewolf pulled on the rope. 'Whoa, Leo. Stop for a sec, calm down.'

Dad hurried over to Grandpa Werewolf,

looking at Leo with awe. Leo was a whopper of a werewolf, at least twice as big as Alfie. Grandpa Werewolf looked tiny beside him.

'Hi, Grandpa. Hi, Leo. Wow, you're even bigger than last time,' Dad said.

Like Alfie, Leo was one of Grandpa Werewolf's grandsons. He lived in the wild and had an unusual way of talking. He looked like a brutal, bloodthirsty beast, but he was quite nice once you got to know him.

'It's lucky to bump into you like this,' Dad said.

Grandpa Werewolf raised his eyebrows at the sight of the flowerpot, diving mask and fur coat. 'Um, yeah, I was wondering where you'd got to. Fortunately I was able to find Leo quite quickly. He'd already changed into a wolf so I lent him a raincoat and a cap.'

'Have you found Alfie's track?' asked Dad.

Grandpa Werewolf nodded. 'We went to your house, but you'd already left so we started track tracing straightaway.'

'And that rope?' asked Mum.

Grandpa grimaced. 'I'm not that fast any more. I can't keep up with Leo without it.'

The big wolf growled. 'Let's be on our wayses, Grandpa. Leo's smelling little werewolf all loud-and-clearsy. Not that little werewolf has BOs or any stink like that.'

Grandpa Werewolf nodded. He was still panting from running so much. Beads of sweat gleamed on his snout.

'What are you doing here anyway?'

Quickly, Dad explained what had happened.

'Ah, of course,' said Grandpa softly. 'Noura is a track tracer too. I didn't think of her.'

Tim couldn't bear it any longer. 'Can we get going? Grandpa Werewolf can come in the car.'

Mum nodded. 'Good idea. Come on, Grandpa. Someone your age shouldn't be running behind youngsters with a rope around his waist.' She undid the knot.

'I agree,' said Tim's father.

'That's more up my husband's street,' Mum continued. 'He loves doing unusual things.'

'Exactly!' said Dad. 'I mean . . . huh?'

Mum tied the rope around Dad's stomach. 'Come on, William. If we lose Leo, we'll never find Alfie. So you have to keep your eye on him. And anyway, a bit of running is

good for your belly. You could do with losing a few pounds. I'll drive. Grandpa, Tim, get into the car. Leo, seek Alfie!'

'But . . .' said Dad. 'Whoops!' He flew forwards. Leo had torn off and was pulling Dad along behind him.

Mum jumped in behind the steering wheel, started the car and revved the engine. 'Hold on, everyone!' she shouted. She put it into gear and put her foot down.

The car jolted forward, then stalled.

23

Get Lost!

Noura's mouth fell open. 'Why are you acting so weird, Alfie?'

'I'm not acting weird. I just want you to go away. Now! You're not wanted here.' Alfie glanced quickly at Uncle Seb's shack. It was still dark.

Noura's damp eyes gleamed. 'What are you saying, Alfie?'

'You heard me, Noura. Get out of here. Go away! I don't want to see you here again!'

Noura let go of the bars and stepped back in astonishment.

Valentine nodded approvingly. 'Well done,' he whispered. 'I think she got the message.'

Alfie didn't answer. Noura looked completely distraught. Tears were shining in her eyes. She didn't understand at all.

Alfie could hardly bear it, but he didn't have time to feel sorry. He had to send her away, even if it hurt. Every second Noura stayed here put her in danger.

'Go now!' he growled in a quavery voice. 'Get out of here. Get lost, will you?'

Noura turned around. She hung her head and slunk off, looking back one last time.

Alfie almost burst into tears himself. Noura let out one quiet sob, then walked on.

'I don't mean it, Noura,' whispered Alfie.

He looked over to Valentine. 'Was that right, do you think?'

Valentine gave him the thumbs-up. 'Fine. Very good for a beginner. That's the way to lose your girlfriend for ever.' He laughed a grim little laugh.

'But that's not what I want!' exclaimed

Alfie. 'I don't want to lose her for ever!'

'Tough,' said Valentine. 'Now you don't have a girlfriend any more. Just like me.'

Suddenly Noura screamed. Something metallic flashed near her hind leg. She collapsed in a heap and lay writhing on the ground.

'Noura!' shouted Alfie, tugging helplessly at the bars.

'What is it? Please, say something.'

But Noura could only groan with pain.

'Wolf trap,' said Valentine. 'Silvertooth has put out a few traps and snares here and there. Your ex-girlfriend just stood on one.'

Suddenly the light turned on in the shack.

24

Road Rage

Mum had got the car started again. 'Drive, you stupid thing!' she shouted.

The engine throbbed with fear as the car jolted and jerked down the street, throwing Grandpa Werewolf backwards and forwards on the back seat.

'Do you even have a driving licence?'

Mum had her eyes fixed on the road in front of her and was holding the steering wheel tight with both hands. 'Not really, Grandpa, but I've sat next to my husband often enough to see how it's done.'

She tried to accelerate for the third time and for the third time the car stalled and rolled to a halt. Immediately other cars started beeping their horns.

'Yeah, yeah, take it easy, will you?' said Mum. 'I'll just start it again.' She turned the key.

The engine gave a tired squeal, then died again, leaving the car as stationary as a house in the middle of the road.

'Watch out!' Tim shouted.

A big lorry loomed up towards them. Mum stamped on the brake, even though she didn't need to. The lorry braked too and slid sideways over the road with its tyres squealing and its brakes screeching, finally stopping just in front of Mum's car.

There were big yellow letters on the side of the lorry: RCUPA.

'Big fat idiot!' Mum shouted, winding down her window and sticking out her head. 'I had right of way.'

A man with grey hair and reflective sunglasses looked down through the side window of the lorry. 'But you weren't going anywhere!' he said.

'So what? Right of way is right of way. Maybe you should take off those mirror glasses, then you might be able to see who should give way to who.'

'Now now,' said Grandpa Werewolf quietly, 'You're being a tad aggressive, aren't you?'

But Mum wasn't listening. 'Get out of the way, you great big bully with your great big lorry! We're in a hurry!'

The lorry driver's face turned bright red. 'There's obviously no point in talking to you. I'm going.' He wound up his window and started the engine.

'Hurry up,' mumbled Tim. 'Hurry up. We've already lost Noura. Now we're going to lose Dad and Leo too.'

25

Caught!

Noura groaned and thrashed back and forth before giving up and lying motionless. Her leg was caught in an iron trap.

Alfie rattled the bars of his cage, looking over at the light now shining from the shack. 'We have to do something. We have to do something. What can we do?'

Valentine stared at him. 'There's nothing we can do. It's too bad, but your ex-girlfriend is a goner. Hopefully Silvertooth won't shoot her dead, but he might. Then you won't even have an ex-girlfriend any more. Just like me.

I don't have an ex-girlfriend either.'

Alfie whimpered with misery. 'Will he really shoot her dead?'

Valentine shrugged. 'You never know with Silvertooth.'

The shack door opened and Uncle Seb came out with his gun and a big torch. He scanned the grounds, then shone it straight at Noura, summing up the situation in a glance. 'Ah, what have we here? A surprise.

Another werewolf. And this one walked into my trap just like that, of its own free will. I'm sure Dr Cutter will be willing to pay even more for a girl werewolf.' Silvertooth was so happy he lit up a cigar.

For a moment, Alfie was relieved. At least Uncle Seb wasn't going to shoot Noura. She was worth good money.

'You creep! You and your stupid ideas,' he hissed at Valentine.

'I'm sorry,' Valentine smirked. 'I'm sorry Silvertooth's not going to shoot her dead.'

Alfie could only grit his teeth and watch as Uncle Seb rolled an empty cage over to Noura.

There is no Uncle Seb, he thought. That man is just a crook called Silvertooth.

Silvertooth released the trap and picked Noura up by the scruff of her neck. She hung limply from his hand and remained motionless, even after he'd put her in the cage.

'Don't pretend, wolf,' he said. 'That trap wasn't even sharp. You're not even bleeding.

There was just a bit of silver in it. I wouldn't want to damage the goods. You're worth a lot more in one piece.'

He rolled the cage over to the others and stood it upright next to Alfie's. 'Here, werewolf, now you've got some company. Not for long though, because the collectors should be here any minute.' He sniggered and blew a cloud of smoke through the bars. Alfie started coughing, but Silvertooth didn't care. 'My customers will be delighted with this extra werewolf cub.'

Suddenly the Scoffle started screeching.

'Thunderation!' roared Silvertooth. 'What did I tell you? Shut your gob, monster! If a buyer doesn't show up for you soon, I'll have you fried on toast.' He gave the Scoffle's box a furious kick, turned and strode back to the shack.

The box shivered for a moment. The long tail flicked out through the bars of the door and smacked hard against the ground. The growling, crunching sound of grinding teeth came from inside the cage.

Then it fell silent again.

'Noura!' whispered Alfie. 'Are you OK? I didn't mean any of those things I said. I had to say that to get you to go. I was trying to protect you. This is just what I was trying to avoid. Please say something.'

But Noura didn't answer. She just lay on the floor of the cage as motionless as a rug.

26

Which Way?

The lorry had driven off, but a long line of beeping cars had built up behind theirs. Mum tried to restart it.

'Hurry up, Mum!' Tim said. 'I can't see Dad and Leo anywhere any more.'

'Don't worry, son. I'll catch 'em.'

The car went *vroom*, blowing a big cloud of black smoke out of the exhaust pipe.

'I did it!' Mum cried. 'Buckle up and we're off. Which way did they go?'

Tim pointed into the darkness in front of

them. 'Somewhere in that direction. Straight ahead.'

'OK,' Mum said. 'I'll just drive straight ahead then.'

She accelerated very carefully and the car drove off very slowly. This time it didn't stall.

'It's going better already,' said Grandpa Werewolf. 'You're a fast learner, a real star!'

Mum smiled proudly and sped up a little. 'Are we still going in the right direction? Should we go left, right or straight ahead?'

Grandpa Werewolf leant forward over the back of the front seat. 'Wait a sec. There's something on the road in front of us. Maybe . . .'

'What do you mean?' Mum asked. 'Those droppings? That's nothing. It just means a horse has been this way.'

Grandpa smiled. 'That's where you're mistaken. Do you remember the story of Hansel and Gretel? They left a trail of breadcrumbs so they could find their way home.'

Mum smiled. 'Breadcrumbs? I think you must have hit your head too hard, Grandpa. You're all mixed up. They're definitely not breadcrumbs.'

Grandpa shook his head. 'I know they're

not breadcrumbs. But Leo is smarter than you think. He's done the same kind of thing as Hansel and Gretel. He's left something to show us the way. It's just not breadcrumbs!'

Mum looked at Grandpa with big eyes. 'Oh, now I get it. You mean to say that Leo . . . That what's lying there in the road isn't horse droppings, but werewolf droppings?'

Grandpa Werewolf nodded. 'Exactly. Leo has left us a clue. Follow that poo!'

27

Dead?

Alfie looked fearfully at Noura. She still hadn't moved. Silvertooth was back in his shack. He hadn't given her a second glance.

'Noura, say something,' Alfie pleaded.

Valentine stared at the black werewolf. 'Don't be such a werewimp! It's no big deal. She's just fainted. From the fright, I guess.'

Alfie nodded.

'Either that or she's dead,' Valentine said. 'No big deal either.'

Alfie threw himself up against the bars and lashed out at Valentine with his claws. 'What?

How dare you say something like that, you stupid vampire?'

Valentine shrugged. 'It's a joke. It's just a vampire joke to cheer you up. Being dead is totally normal for vampires. I'm dead too, more or less. It's called un-dead.'

With a sad sigh, Alfie sat down again and picked up Tim's bear. 'Poor Noura. It's all my fault. It's my fault she turned into a werewolf. It's my fault she's in a cage. And it's my fault she's unconscious. She just wanted to rescue me. I'm nothing but bad luck.'

Valentine let out a snort of laughter. 'Come on, don't be so pathetic. You've got a friend who's crazy about you *and* you've got a girlfriend who comes to rescue you. They'd only do that if they loved you. What are you complaining about bad luck for?' He wiped his eyes. 'You were born lucky. You just have some unfortunate moments. Now me, I don't have anyone. I can't bear daylight. And I have to live off blood. Want to swap?'

Alfie looked at Valentine. 'You're right, Valentine. I'm a whinger. I—'

Suddenly the Scoffle let out an enormous screech.

Noura blinked. 'What was that?'

'Noura!' growled Alfie. 'Are you OK?'

The black werewolf looked up. 'What happened? Where am I?'

Alfie jumped up and down with excitement. He grabbed hold of the bars. 'You stood on a trap, Noura. Made of silver. And now you've been captured, just like me.'

Noura scrambled up on to her feet. 'Oh yeah, now I remember.' She shook her head and looked at Alfie. Her voice turned gloomy. 'You sent me away. You told me to get lost.'

Alfie reached out to her through the bars. 'I didn't mean it like that, Noura. We've been captured by Silvertooth. We're trapped. That's why I sent you away. I didn't want you to get caught too. And Valentine said that being mean was the best way to get you to go, so—'

'Sure, blame me, why don't you?' blurted the vampire, turning away angrily and creeping off to the back of his cage.

Noura stretched her foreleg out and took Alfie's paw. 'It will all work out, Alfie. Tim and his parents are coming to rescue you.'

Alfie shook his head. 'Tim? He doesn't even know where I am.'

'Yes, he does,' Noura said. 'We came looking for you together. I was the track tracer. They'll be here any minute now.'

Alfie looked at the motionless bushes. The forest was dark and silent. 'What's keeping them then?'

Noura scratched her throat. 'They were right behind me. At least, I thought they were. Maybe . . .'

Her face fell.

'Oh, how stupid of me,' she said, sitting down on the floor of her cage. 'I didn't pay attention. Once I smelt your track I just kept on running. I guess they weren't able to keep up.'

Alfie looked at her with a concerned expression. 'Does your paw still hurt, Noura?'

'No, it's fine. I hardly notice it.'

Suddenly they heard a racket coming

from between the trees. Branches snapped, bushes rustled.

'What's that?' whispered Noura.

Alfie felt cold all over. The Scoffle suddenly stopped snoring. A frightened cry went up from Valentine's cage.

'The collectors are coming!'

28

'Trapded!'

Leo and Tim's father were hiding in the bushes. Dad was still panting from running so much. He wasn't a little bit tired – he was totally knackered. The diving mask was halfway down his nose. The flowerpot was perched at an angle on top of his head.

'You see that, Leo?' he panted. 'Those cages over there. You think that's Alfie?'

The wolf nodded his enormous head.

'Leo knows it for certains, least he thinks he does. Leo's been smelling little cuz and that smell be going arrowsy straight bashkerbumps right to those cagers.'

Dad wiped the sweat from his forehead and straightened his diving mask. 'Why did you have to run so fast, Leo? Even our car couldn't keep up with you.'

Leo grinned. His razor-sharp teeth gleamed white in the shade of his cap. 'Don't youse worry, Dadsy. Leo be leaving number twos in drips and drops along the way. And one more just before we's going into this forest.'

'Yes, I smelt that,' Dad sighed.

Leo beamed with pride. 'Good, huh? They's be finding us in jiffies. Leo drops one here too.'

He lifted up his raincoat.

'No, wait!' Dad exclaimed. 'That's really not necessary.'

But Leo winked. 'All taken care of, Dadsy.'

Dad pinched his nose shut. 'Now I'm a track tracer too, I suppose.'

Leo tugged on Dad's sleeve. 'Now now, Dadsy, let your nose go. We's going to rescuefy little Alfie.' He stepped out of the bushes.

Dad hurried out after him. 'Wait, Leo, don't rush into it. We have to be careful. That horrible Silvertooth is probably over there in that house. We have to be careful. Let's wait for the others first.'

'No waitsies! Bam, wham, kaboom! Dadsy and Leo rescue little cuz wolf. Everyone be proud as punches. Dadsy and Leo be heroes. Mumsy glad. Tim glad. Grandpa Werewolf glad. Cuz wolf Alfie gladdest of all.'

'But, Leo, just wait a—' Dad fell silent when he stood on something.

Click.

'What was that?' whispered Dad. 'I heard a clicking noise.'

Leo shrugged.

Swish, swish, swish.

Dad looked up and down, left and right. 'And that was a swishing sound.'

All around them, something shot up from on the ground. It had been spread under their feet. A concealed net.

Now it closed in a flash around Leo
and Dad.

Whoosh, whoosh.

Above them a draw cord pulled tight
automatically. The whole thing shot up into
the air. It was tied to a branch with a rope.
Suddenly Leo and Dad were hanging high
above the ground.

'Wow!' Dad said. 'Just like bungee jumping
upside down.'

Leo growled and kicked. 'We's trapped!
Oh, the dastardly disasterer. Silvertooth
has catched us in his nets like two little
bunny-hoppers.' He roared and tore with his
claws and bit with his teeth, but the net was
too strong.

Dad shrieked.

'Oh, sorry, Dadsy,' Leo said. 'I's not seeing
your finger.'

Helpless, they dangled from the tree
like fish in a net.

29

Dr Cutter

'Left here,' said Grandpa Werewolf.

Mum turned the wheel, then stamped on the brake. Everyone shot forward and the engine stalled. They'd come to the end of the road, which continued into the forest as a track.

'Are you sure we have to go in here?'

Grandpa Werewolf nodded. 'Absolutely. Look. Leo's left a sign for us right in front of that path.'

Mum peered through the windscreen at Leo's sign, which was lit up by the car's headlights and plain to see. Tim looked over Mum's shoulder. 'Are you sure it's Leo's?'

Grandpa Werewolf nodded. 'No two poos are the same, Tim. I'd recognize a werewolf poo at a hundred metres. That's definitely what it is and it's a very special one. And it's Leo's, as sure as I'm sitting here.'

Mum undid her seat belt and got out of the car to study the poo more closely. It was shaped like an arrow and it pointed straight into the forest.

'Impressive,' Mum mumbled. 'Leo's got talent. OK, everyone get out.'

Tim looked at her with surprise. 'What are we going to do, Mum?'

'We're going to walk. If Alfie is being held captive in this forest, we have to look for him quietly. A car would be much too noisy.'

'You're a smart woman,' said Grandpa Werewolf. 'If I was fifty years younger, I wouldn't think twice.'

Mum giggled for a second, then led them into the forest. Fortunately the full moon was shining through the branches to light the way.

'Where are Dad and Leo?' Tim asked.

Mum laid a hand on his shoulder. 'I bet we bump into them any moment now.'

They followed the path deeper into the forest. Suddenly a voice called out, 'Hello, who's there?' There were figures moving in the moonlight. A little bit further along they could make out the dark shape of a large lorry.

'Grandpa Werewolf, get back,' Mum whispered and right away the old werewolf slipped into the bushes.

'Who's there?'

Two men appeared. One was wearing a brown suit and a brown hat and carrying a case. The other had grey hair and glasses with reflective lenses.

'Mum, that's the guy you told off at the crossing,' Tim said.

'I see that too, son. Just act like you're a babe in the woods.'

'But, Mum, they'll see I'm not a baby.'

'Shhh, Tim, quiet.'

A torch shone full into Mum and Tim's faces.

'Would you please shine that light somewhere else!' Mum snapped in her strictest voice.

'Oh, beg your pardon, ma'am.'

The beam of light went down to the ground.

'Hello,' said the man with the reflective glasses. 'I am Dr Cutter. This is Mr Frogley of the RCUPA.'

Mum gulped. 'The RCUPA? The Reception Centre for Unusual People and Animals?'

'Precisely,' said Dr Cutter. He gave Mum a probing look from over the top of his glasses. One of his eyes was all white, without a pupil.

What a creep, thought Tim.

'Don't I know you from somewhere, ma'am?'

Mum coughed and shook her head. 'Not as far as I know.'

'Hmmm, then it must have been someone

else, someone who looked like you.' Dr Cutter ran his fingers through his grey hair. 'Do you know your way around this forest? You see, we seem to be lost.'

'Oh?' Mum smiled innocently. 'What are you doing here?'

Dr Cutter hesitated for a second. 'Um . . . We're here to pick up some special . . . er, animal species. In a manner of speaking. We have an appointment with Mr. Silvertooth. His Menagerie of Extraordinary Creatures is somewhere in this forest. Mr Frogley here is a purchaser for collectors and I'm a researcher.'

'Oh? And what exactly does a researcher do?'

Dr Cutter cackled with laughter. 'Well, I'm a kind of surgeon. I do operations. I have some very sharp scalpels.'

Tim felt a shiver run down his spine. He squeezed his mother's hand. Then he picked a sturdy branch up off the ground and put it in his mother's other hand behind her back. She squeezed his hand in reply.

'But I don't want to bore you any longer,' Dr Cutter said. 'Do you know which way we have to go to find the menagerie?'

Mum smiled a cold-blooded smile. 'You're right. You don't want to bore me any longer. And you won't.' She swung the thick branch up over her head like a club. Tim dived at Mr Frogley's legs. And suddenly Grandpa Werewolf came roaring out of the bushes.

Unfortunately, he stumbled and fell on his nose.

30

Nutcase

Alfie gripped the bars with two paws. Panting
with surprise, he watched the net swing back
and forth high in the tree.

'Did you see that, Noura? Did you
see those two people walk into that trap?
That net shot up like a rocket as if it was
attached to elastic cables, and the next
moment it was up in the tree. Valentine
said that Silvertooth has got traps all over
the place. We're just lucky it wasn't Tim
and his father.'

'Who are those two?' asked Noura.

Alfie shrugged. 'Collectors, I think, one with a funny hat and one with a cap. I'm not sure though. I didn't get a good look at them. I'm glad they got caught in the trap though.'

Valentine crept back out from his dark corner and peered at the net. 'They're no collectors.'

Alfie frowned at Valentine. 'How do you know?'

'Because one of them's a wolf. A big one. Your kind of wolf.'

'A big werewolf? Are you sure?'

'Yep,' said Valentine. 'We vampires have super sharp eyes.' He squinted and looked again. 'And another very strange character. Someone with a flowerpot on his head. He's wearing a diving mask and he's got blue hair. What a nutcase!'

Alfie looked at Noura. 'Blue hair?'

'A flowerpot and a diving mask?' said Noura.

They looked at each other and growled, 'Tim's dad!' at exactly the same time.

Silvertooth stormed out of his shack with his cigar in his mouth and his gun under one arm. He ran over to the tree and looked up at the net. His catch was still wriggling. A snarling and growling sound came from the net.

'Aha,' Silvertooth cried. 'I thought I heard something. A fine haul by the looks of things. Yet another werewolf. It's good werewolf weather, tonight. The collectors will be overjoyed.' He screwed up his eyes. 'But what's that other one? It's not a werewolf. But it does look like an extraordinary creature. Blue hair, big strange eyes, a furry coat. Maybe it's a bug-eyed blue-crested nincompoop. They're mega-rare.'

'Lets us out, Silvertoothache!' Leo roared. 'Leo eats you ups and spits you out.'

Alfie looked at Noura. 'It's Leo,' he growled. 'Leo and Tim's father.'

Silvertooth gave a loud laugh. 'No werewolf can harm me, big mouth. And you're so stupid you walked straight into my trap. What a fool!'

Suddenly they heard the sound of an engine and wheels spinning. Lights appeared behind the trees. A big lorry was driving straight through the undergrowth and ploughing through the sand. It jolted and bounced ever closer, then stopped with the engine still roaring.

The engine died and the lights dimmed. Then the door swung open. An old man in a white coat climbed out carefully. His hair was grey and he was wearing reflective glasses that caught the moonlight.

31

A Blue-Crested Nincompoop

'Who's that?' whispered Alfie.

Growling softly, Noura walked circles inside her cage. 'A creep.'

Valentine crept forward and wrapped his fingers around the bars. 'A researcher,' he said with a quavering voice. 'They always look like that. Researchers have white coats. Usually with bloodstains on them. Now we've really had it.' Moaning, he crawled back into the shadows at the rear of his cage.

In the cage next to his, the Scoffle woke up with a screech.

Someone else got out of the lorry: brown suit, brown felt hat.

Silvertooth walked up, holding out his hand. 'Dr Cutter?'

The old man nodded and shook Silvertooth's hand.

'Excellent. Then you must be Mr Frogley.'

The other man just nodded.

Silvertooth pointed to the cages. 'Let's not waste any time. Come this way.'

The two visitors followed along behind Silvertooth, stopping in front of Alfie's cage.

'This is the werewolf for you, Dr Cutter. A magnificent specimen.'

Suddenly the Scoffle screeched. Its box shook back and forth. Silvertooth turned a furious red. 'Thunderation! Why don't you just shut up for once, you horrible creature?' He stuck his gun in through the bars and gave the Scoffle a few hard whacks that made it screech again, loudly, then fall silent.

Alfie felt sorry for the Scoffle, even though he'd never seen it.

Silvertooth hung the gun over his shoulder. 'Sorry, doctor. That creature is extremely troublesome. Violence is all it understands and no one wants to buy it off me.' He kicked the box. 'But that's not what we're here for. We're here to talk about this werewolf.'

Dr Cutter looked at Alfie. Alfie stared back at the long wrinkled face with white sideburns. Dr Cutter didn't look mean at all. He actually looked friendly. For a moment he even seemed to be smiling at him. But his eyes stayed hidden behind the reflective glasses.

What a treacherous smile! thought Alfie, baring his teeth and growling.

'Lovely, lovely,' mumbled Dr Cutter.

Silvertooth banged Alfie's cage. 'You can do as much research on him as you like, cut him open or whatever. And that's not all.' He raised a finger in the air and grinned. His silver teeth flashed in the moonlight. 'It's your lucky day, Dr Cutter. Look what I've got here,' he said, walking over to the next cage.

Noura was too scared to look up at the strange doctor.

'Another werewolf,' Silvertooth said. 'A black one, a female. I'll throw her in extra for half price.'

Alfie hurled himself against his bars, growling and snarling. 'Leave Noura alone, you crooks.'

Silvertooth grinned. 'A plucky little werewolf, as you see. What do you say, Dr Cutter?'

The old man nodded. 'Um, yes, of course. The more werewolves the better. I can do lots of lovely operations.'

Silvertooth chuckled. 'But wait. Wait! I've got something else for you. Something very special.' He pointed up. 'Look up there! A whopping great werewolf that I just trapped a minute ago.

'He's yours too, if you'd like him. And I'll throw in that Extraordinary Creature next to him as a free bonus. It's a bug-eyed blue-crested nincompoop.'

Up in the air, Leo growled. He slashed with his claws and lashed out with his legs, making the net dance dangerously in the air.

'Take it easy, Leo,' Dad whispered. 'You're not an acrobat. If you're not careful, we'll fall down.'

Dr Cutter rubbed his hands together.
'Fantastic! Three werewolves and a blue-
crested nincompoop. The more creatures
the better. Load them into the lorry.'

Suddenly Mr Frogley started to cough.
He'd choked on something when he
looked up.

With a contented expression on his face,
Silvertooth lit a cigar. 'Fine. Just drive the
lorry over here.'

Alfie looked at Noura, who was sitting
hunched up in a corner. He could see that
she was trembling. 'Don't give up, Noura,' he
growled. 'We're going to be rescued. I just
don't know how.'

Alfie was trying hard to sound brave, but
inside he didn't feel brave at all. Things were
looking more and more hopeless. If only Tim
was here, he thought. He'd be sure to come
up with a good plan.

Mr Frogley walked over to the lorry.

'Wait, wait,' shouted Silvertooth.

Mr Frogley looked back. 'Is there

something else?'

'You *are* taking the vampire too?' Silvertooth pointed at Valentine's cage.

Mr Frogley swallowed. 'A vampire?'

'Of course,' Silvertooth said. 'That was the agreement. You were picking him up for a collector who wanted a stuffed vampire.'

Mr Frogley coughed. 'Oh yes, that's right. I almost forgot.'

'It doesn't matter,' Valentine cried out in a frightened voice. 'I'll stay here if you don't want to take me. I'd be very difficult to stuff.'

Mr Frogley seemed to think for a moment, then shook his head. 'No, I'd better take you too.'

Alfie had been listening carefully the whole time and it was if his blood was tingling through his veins. There was something about Mr Frogley's voice. He knew that voice. He was sure of it.

Suddenly he heard a sound behind him.

'Pssst, Alfie.'

Surprised, Alfie looked over his shoulder.

There was someone on the other side of his cage, hidden behind a bush.

32

To the Rescue

'Tim!' Alfie whispered, but he was so excited his whisper was too loud. Quickly Silvertooth looked in his direction.

Oops, thought Alfie, he might see Tim. Alfie had recognized Tim by the hair sticking up over the bush. Just then Dr Cutter started coughing loudly.

Silvertooth turned back to the doctor. 'Is my cigar bothering you?'

Still coughing, Dr Cutter shook his head.

Silvertooth patted him on the back. 'Shall we get down to business then, doctor?'

They took a few steps away from the cages.

Even though Alfie was overjoyed to have Tim so close at hand, he was still too scared to move a millimetre.

'Don't look back,' Tim whispered. 'We've come to rescue you.'

'I've still got your favourite bear, Tim. I knew you'd come.' Tears leapt into Alfie's eyes. 'Noura, I told you, didn't I? We're going to be rescued. Tim is here.'

Noura did her best to look back without being noticed and when she saw Tim, her eyes gleamed. Valentine saw him now too.

'Who's that?' he hissed to Alfie.

'That's Tim, my best friend. He's come to rescue us.'

'Oh, great!' Valentine groaned. 'Now his friend's come to rescue him too.'

'Tim,' Noura said under her breath. 'How are you going to rescue us?'

Tim crawled a bit closer to the cages. He had pulled a bush out of the ground and was holding it up in front of him. 'Mum is disguised as Mr Frogley.'

Alfie growled softly. 'I knew it! I recognized her voice.'

'And you see Dr Cutter? You'll never guess who that is.'

Alfie looked at the cruel doctor. 'Who?'

'Grandpa Werewolf.'

'What?' Just in time Alfie clapped a hairy paw over his mouth. 'How can he be, Tim?'

Tim rustled his bush softly. 'Mum knocked them both out. You should have seen it. And Grandpa took on human form again for the first time in ten years. Just to rescue you, Alfie.'

Alfie swallowed.

'But he can't keep it up for long,' Tim said. 'He could turn back into a wolf any moment, so we have to hurry.'

Mr Frogley manoeuvred the lorry very carefully in between the cages. 'There, we can load 'em up.'

Silvertooth chuckled approvingly. 'I hope you're satisfied, Dr Cutter. I'm sure we'll be able to do business again in the future.'

In its cage the Scoffle growled ominously.

'Shut up, beast.' Silvertooth kicked its box, then looked back at Dr Cutter. The doctor's nose seemed to have grown a little. There was more hair on his face too and his ears were a little pointier.

'Are you feeling all right, doctor? You suddenly look a little . . . different.'

Dr Cutter shook his head. 'I'm right as rain. Let's go. Load those cages.'

Suddenly they heard voices. Two men emerged from the bushes. They were in their underwear, stumbling and leaning on each other for support.

'Oh, no,' groaned Tim behind his bush.

'What is it?' said Alfie. 'Who are they?'

Tim groaned again. 'They're the real Dr Cutter and Mr Frogley.'

33

Impostors!

The two men were shivering. Their bare arms and legs were blue from the cold and covered with goosebumps.

High in the air, Leo kicked and roared in the net. The branch they were dangling from bent lower and lower.

'Take it easy, Leo,' Tim's father moaned. 'It hurts every time you move.'

He was bent double with one knee under his chin. The cords of the net pressed his nose flat and cut into his cheeks. His right ear was folded forward. He peered out of the

154

corner of his eye through the diving mask. 'What's happening down there? Who are those two men in their underwear?'

Leo wasn't listening. He tugged on the net and wriggled and bit it harder and harder, but just got more and more tangled.

Meanwhile Silvertooth had turned his gun on the men. 'Who are you? What are you doing here?'

The men pointed at Mum and Grandpa, who were still in disguise.

'Im-p-p-postors!' they stuttered in chorus.

The older man had grey hair and one white pupil-less eye. The other one had an enormous bump on his forehead.

'Th-those two are imp-p-p-postors. They stole my g-g-glasses. And our c-c-clothes.'

Silvertooth looked at the lorry with astonishment. Mum and Grandpa smiled and shrugged.

'Two shivering charlatans in their smalls,' Mum said in her Mr Frogley voice. 'Free-range loonies.'

'L-l-lies!' shouted the old man. 'We're C-C-C-Cutter and F-f-frogley. Th-th-they attacked us! They even stole our t-t-t-t-trousers.' He rubbed his cold blue arms. 'U-use your eyes! Th-the old one's not even hu-hu-human. He's a w-w-werewolf too.

And the other one's a l-l-l-l-lady. She c-c-c-clubbed us with a b-b-b-branch.'

The cigar fell out of Silvertooth's mouth. 'What?'

Again the Scoffle growled in its cage.

'A werewolf?' cried Silvertooth, quickly jabbing his gun in between the bars. The Scoffle snorted furiously, then fell silent.

'Ooh, now we're in for it,' Tim said. 'Grandpa Werewolf can't keep it up much longer.'

Silvertooth had noticed now too. Snorting with rage he strode over to the fake Dr Cutter. The doctor's face had changed. He now had a hairy muzzle and pointy ears. The reflective glasses fell to the ground.

'A-ha!' Silvertooth roared. 'Impostor, you're not Cutter! Now I see. I know you from the old days. I should have blown you away then. Don't think you can make a monkey out of me, old werewolf.' He pointed his gun at Grandpa. 'I think I'll shoot some nice holes in you right now.'

'Run, Grandpa, run!' Alfie screamed. He

157

threw himself against the bars but they were too strong.

Silvertooth pointed at the fake Mr Frogley. 'You there. I'm wondering who you really are.' He reached out with one hand and tore the hat off 'Mr Frogley's' head. Suddenly Mr Frogley had shoulder-length hair. Everyone could see that it was Tim's mother, and everyone could hear it too.

'Shoot if you dare, you sickening Silvertooth!'

Silvertooth grinned and took aim. 'My pleasure, lady.'

'No!' screamed Alfie, throwing himself against the bars again. It was a desperate leap, and Alfie put all his strength and all his fear into it. That made a difference and the cage tilted and toppled, slamming into Silvertooth's back.

With a bang the gun went off . . .

34

Almost Free . . .

The shot echoed through the forest as the silver bullet whistled out of the barrel of the gun, going straight up, just missing Tim's father's nose, and drilling right through the branch the net was tied to. Tim's father shrieked with fright. There was a loud crack.

Silvertooth looked up, dazed, from where he was sitting on the ground. 'Whoops,' he mumbled. 'I almost hit the blue-crested nincompoop.'

Grandpa Werewolf and Tim's mother

looked up too.

A moment later everyone was looking up and everyone was holding their breath. The branch bent lower and lower. Tim's father screamed and Leo roared. Then the branch snapped and fell. The net ripped open where Leo had finally gnawed through it and they both came tumbling down like ripe apples.

First the thick branch hit Silvertooth on the head, then Leo landed on top of him. And then Tim's father landed on top of Leo, leaving all three of them sprawled on the ground. Tim's father and Leo lay there groaning. Silvertooth was out cold.

Just then a small bush rushed forward. A hand poked out through the leaves to grab the bunch of keys on Silvertooth's belt. Then the bush shuffled over to Alfie's cage. The cage was still lying on its side.

'Alfie, I've got the key.'

'Quick, then.'

Tim tried a key. 'Help, this one doesn't fit.'

He tried another, but that didn't fit either. Finally he found the right key. The lock clicked open and Alfie was free. He climbed out of the cage.

'Look, Tim,' he growled. 'Here's your teddy bear. I kept it safe for you.'

A few seconds later Noura was free too. She gave Alfie a big hug.

'What about me?' Valentine shouted. 'Don't forget me, Alfie the Werewolf. After all, I'm your second-best friend. Aren't I?'

Alfie looked around. Silvertooth was lying stretched out on the ground, motionless. Leo and Tim's father stood up unsteadily.

Tim's mother ran over to her husband with her arms spread wide. There were two starbursts in his diving mask. 'Thank goodness, sweetheart, nothing's broken except the glass.'

Leo staggered around dizzily. 'Leo's whamsied on the ground. Now Leo's head be aching over and out. Ooh, it all be turning black as the blackest blotterer. Byesie-bye!' Leo fell over, unconscious too.

Grandpa Werewolf was looking a little dazed. 'This is all too fast and furious for an old wolf like me.'

The real Dr Cutter and Mr Frogley were still shivering.

'Give me my clothes back,' shouted the real Dr Cutter.

'Mine too,' shouted the real Mr Frogley.

Silvertooth cautiously opened one eye. No one noticed.

'Have you hurt yourself, dear?' Tim's mother asked, checking her husband over from head to toe.

'Let me out, quick,' begged Valentine. 'Then we can all go home.'

Very slowly, Silvertooth opened his other eye. There was still no one paying him any attention. Everyone was too busy shouting and talking.

'When are you going to let me out?' cried Valentine.

Alfie didn't say a word. He just looked into Noura's brown, gold-flecked eyes. 'That was brave of you, coming to rescue me.'

Noura smiled. 'I—'

'Shut up, all of you!' Silvertooth leapt up suddenly. He'd already grabbed his gun. 'Enough,' he roared.

Tim's hand went up to his head. 'Oh, stupid, stupid, stupid! I should have grabbed the gun when he was knocked out.'

Silvertooth had a crazed look in his eyes. 'I've got the gun, so you have to do what I say. In the old days I killed tons of werewolves and now I feel like killing some more. All you werewolves line up next to each other. Now! And then I'll shoot some nice holes in you.'

35

Bang!

Noura held on tight to Alfie.

'Are things going to go wrong now, after all?' she asked anxiously.

Tim's father straightened his diving mask and marched up to Silvertooth with his hands on his hips. Because of the cracks in the glass of the diving mask he couldn't see a thing. He walked right past Silvertooth and started talking to a tree. 'Now listen here, Silvertooth. Enough's enough. We—'

Bang! Dad stopped talking. Silvertooth

had bashed him on the flowerpot with his gun.

'I told you to shut up, blabbermouth! You're not even a bug-eyed blue-crested nincompoop. You're another impostor.'

The pot fell to the ground in two pieces.

'You monster! How dare you hit my husband!' shouted Tim's mother. 'And how dare you call him a blabbermouth! That's my job! Plus, you're the impostor. You're not Alfie's uncle at all!'

'My poor, poor, pot hat . . .' Dad stuttered. 'What a waste!' He wobbled. It was as if he could suddenly hear birds singing.

'Shut your traps, both of you,' said Silvertooth. 'Stand there and don't say a word. I've had enough. I'm going to shoot holes in werewolves.'

'You and your shooting,' Tim's mother said. 'Stop it right now. You'd think we were in a cowboy film.'

The real Dr Cutter stepped forward. 'Silvertooth, my good man, restrain yourself, please. We don't want a bloodbath here, do we? That kind of thing should be done properly in a dissecting room.'

Silvertooth looked at Dr Cutter. Even his eyes had taken on a silver gleam. He shook his head. 'You don't get it. You're just a nut in undies. I'm Sebarino Silvertooth, the terror of all werewolves. These specimens have made a monkey out of me. That's why I am now very keen on shooting holes in werewolves. Just like I used to in the good old days. So get out of the way, Cutter, unless you'd like a nice silver bullet . . . right between the eyes.'

Dr Cutter ran back to Mr Frogley. 'He's gone mad. Completely mad!'

Silvertooth gave a nasty laugh. 'Let's see. Who gets to go first?' He looked at Alfie. 'Ah, my so-called nephew, of course. I've got a lovely little present for you here, made of silver.'

'*Wrow*, I'm not your nephew,' growled Alfie. 'And I don't want any presents. I just want to go home.'

Silvertooth spat on the ground. 'Tough

luck, werewolf.'

'Don't shoot!' screamed Tim's mother.

Tim's father was still swaying. The blow on his flowerpot had made him go a bit cross-eyed. He kept saying, 'Tweet, tweet. Where are the birds?'

Silvertooth ignored them and brought the gun up to his shoulder. Slowly he aimed it at Alfie.

'No!' growled Noura, quickly jumping in front of Alfie. Without so much as blinking, she stared straight at Silvertooth.

'Fine by me,' said Silvertooth. 'You can go first.'

36

One Last Wish

'No!' cried Mum quickly stepping in front of Noura.

'Tweet, tweet!' said Dad, pushing his wife out of the way.

In its box the Scoffle yowled. Silvertooth lowered his gun. 'Thunder and botheration!' he roared. 'We're not here to play musical chairs. Stop it and stand still for once. I'm dying to get a good shot in.'

He took aim again, but now Grandpa Werewolf moved over in front of Dad. 'Aim at me then, Silvertooth. I'm already old.'

'Whatever,' snarled Silvertooth. 'I'm finally going to get to you, you old pain in the neck.'

'No, Grandpa,' cried Alfie, running forward and leaping in front of Grandpa Werewolf.

Silvertooth aimed at Alfie, but in the same instant a bush shuffled in between the two of them.

'What's happening now?' screamed Silvertooth.

Noura immediately leapt in front of the bush, and so it went on. Mum. Dad. Bush. Grandpa. Noura. Alfie. And finally Leo joined in too. He'd regained consciousness.

'Is this game for everyones?' he cried, pushing Alfie aside and taking front position. 'Leo be IT. Shoots at Leo, Silvertoothache.'

The real Dr Cutter and Mr Frogley stood there gaping. The spectacle was so exciting they'd both warmed up.

'These are all extremely Extraordinary Creatures,' Mr Frogley whispered. 'I want them all for the RCUPA. Especially that one with the flowerpot. Have you ever seen anything like it, Dr Cutter?'

Valentine watched silently from inside his cage, tears streaming over his pale cheeks. 'They all love each other so much,' he said. 'If only I had a family like this.'

Silvertooth stamped his foot. 'You're driving me mad! Stark raving mad! But now I've had enough. I'll just blow you all away.' Again he aimed his gun at Alfie.

This can't go on like this, thought Alfie. This madman really is going to shoot someone.

'Any last wishes, nephew?'

An angry howl sounded from the Scoffle's box. Alfie's mind raced.

'Um, yes, I do have a last wish.' Slowly he shuffled sideways towards the box. 'Can I stand here when you shoot me?'

The others shuffled over after Alfie. Silvertooth roared with laughter.

'What a ridiculous wish. You're all mad. Why would you want to stand there?'

Alfie looked at the Scoffle's box. The

tip of its tail flicked out through the bars of the door.

'Um, the light's better here, Mr. Silvertooth.'

Alfie shuffled a little bit further until he was close to the box. Everyone else followed him.

'Stop. That's far enough! You're not trying to escape, are you? Not a chance, werewolf cub.'

A couple of strides brought Silvertooth up to Alfie. He was standing with his back to

the Scoffle's box. He didn't hear the rumbling behind him, where something was bumping. Where something was stamping and knocking and swishing its tail.

Silvertooth didn't look over his shoulder. He leered down the barrel of his gun. The tip of his tongue poked out between his lips. He closed one eye. 'Say bye-bye, Alfie.'

He didn't see what was happening behind him, but the others did. The Scoffle's cage was moving, sliding back and forth, rocking a little, even tilting up off the ground.

'I don't think so,' growled Alfie. 'Look behind you.'

37

The Scoffle

Silvertooth laughed. 'That's an old trick. Do you expect me to fall for that?'

Behind him there was a rumbling noise and a deep belly growl that made Silvertooth turn around after all. He shrieked with surprise as the Scoffle's long tail shot out and wrapped around his legs.

Whack! With enormous force the Scoffle pulled Silvertooth right through the bars and into the small box. *Bang!* The door shattered into little pieces. *Crack!*

Then there was total silence. No one

moved. They all just stared at the Scoffle's cage.

'What was that?' whispered Noura.

'The Scoffle,' growled Alfie. 'I think it's a bit angry with Silvertooth and I'm not surprised, after all the times he's hit it.'

Something snapped inside the Scoffle's cage and then Silvertooth's gun came flying out broken into two pieces with a knot in the barrel. The next moment something else came flying out. Two silver teeth. Then nothing. Just a loud burp inside the cage. Somewhere far away in the forest an owl shrieked. Valentine broke the silence.

'D'you see that!' he cried. 'The Scoffle ate him up. Just like I said. It's as small as a cat, but it can eat a whole elephant if it needs to. That was really smart thinking, Alfie, luring Silvertooth into the Scoffle's claws.'

Alfie blushed. 'I didn't know what else to do, but I didn't mean it to eat Silvertooth. I just wanted . . .' He sighed deeply and fell silent.

Grandpa Werewolf laid a paw on Alfie's

shoulder. 'You didn't have any choice, Alfie.
It was Silvertooth's own fault.'

Everyone stared disbelievingly at the cage
that had swallowed up Silvertooth. Almost
everyone, at least. Dr Cutter and Mr Frogley
had slipped into the cab of the lorry.

'Drive, Frogley,' said Dr Cutter.

'What about our clothes?' exclaimed
Mr Frogley.

'Forget 'em. Get us out of here before they
feed *us* to that creature as well!'

Frogley started the engine and drove off quickly.

A peaceful snoring was now coming from the broken cage. The Scoffle was sleeping soundly after its savoury snack. Tim's mother walked over to Alfie and hugged him with tears in her eyes. 'Oh, son, for a while there I was scared we'd never see you again.'

Then Noura and Grandpa Werewolf and Leo hugged him too. Dad hugged a bush, thinking it was Tim, but Tim was inside the bush that Alfie was hugging. Everyone was very happy.

'What a family,' said Valentine, who was still locked in his cage. 'I wish I had one like that.' Once again he was so moved that tears ran down his cheeks. 'Can you let me out of here? Then everyone can go home. And maybe someone will give me a hug too.'

Grandpa Werewolf gave a deep sigh. 'That sounds like a very good idea. Going home, I mean. But what do we do with the Scoffle?'

'Well,' said Tim's father. 'I think it's a pretty cool animal. Unusual, I mean. For now it can live at our house. In the shed, maybe. That's different. I mean, compared to a guinea pig or a hamster.'

38

An Unexpected Visitor

The next few weeks flew by and soon everything was back to normal. Tim, his parents and Alfie were watching TV. It was evening and Noura had come to visit.

Tim had his teddy bear next to him on the chair and couldn't stop smiling. Every now and then he'd sneak a glance at Alfie and his smile would grow even wider. Alfie didn't know why.

Suddenly Dad coughed and looked at Mum. 'Ahem, shall we tell Alfie then?'

Mum nodded and Tim nodded along with

her, his head going all the way up and down. He was beaming.

Alfie looked at Noura. 'What are they talking about?'

She shrugged.

'It's like this, Alfie,' Mum said. 'We—'

Just then the doorbell rang.

'I'll get it,' Alfie said, running into the hall and opening the front door. To his surprise there was no one there. 'Strange!' Alfie mumbled and was about to shut the door when he heard a familiar voice.

'Wait a sec, wait a sec. I'm coming.'

Two shoes appeared at the top of the doorway. Someone was coming down out of the sky. Alfie stood there gaping as the shoes slowly descended, revealing thin white ankles . . . then two trouser legs, a black cape and white hands . . . and a pale face with spiky yellow hair.

'Valentine!' Alfie exclaimed.

The vampire landed softly on the ground, baring his sharp fangs in a big grin. 'Hi, Alfie. Can I come in?'

'Sure! I mean, at least, as long as you promise not to be mean to anyone.'

'I promise.'

Alfie stepped aside. 'Come in then. Nice. Can you fly? I didn't know that!'

Valentine wrapped his cloak around him. 'Of course! All vampires can fly. Unless they're locked in a cage, at least. This is my special flying cloak.'

Alfie led Valentine into the living room. 'Look who's here!'

Everyone said hello and the vampire's pale face blushed red for a moment. Most people ran away the moment they saw him.

'Um, hello, everyone. How are you and how's the Scoffle doing?'

'Fantastic,' said Dad. 'The Scoffle too. It's easy to look after and very shy. We're still not sure exactly what it looks like. It sleeps all day rolled up in a ball in its box in the shed.'

'It might have started hibernating,' Alfie said. 'And even if it hasn't, it hasn't eaten anyone yet. We're going to let it stay until spring and then we'll think about it, won't we, Mum?'

Mum nodded. 'That's right. Have a seat, Valentine. Would you like a glass of . . . um . . . tomato juice. I don't have any blood. Not cold, anyway.'

Valentine roared with laughter. 'You're so much fun. I wish I had a family like this. I . . .' Suddenly he looked serious. 'But I've come about something completely different.'

Alfie looked at him. 'What do you mean, Valentine? Why have you come?'

'Well,' the vampire said. 'I wanted to show you something. I've brought Silvertooth with me.'

'What?' cried Alfie, jumping up.

39

Silverteeth

Everyone stared disbelievingly at Valentine.

'You've brought Silvertooth with you? How? The Scoffle ate him up, didn't it? We thought it did. Were we wrong?'

Noura fronted up to Valentine. 'What are you playing at now? Are you trying to scare Alfie again? That's not funny, you know.'

Valentine smiled. 'Really, I'm not lying.' He stuck his hand in under his cloak. 'I've got more than just one silver tooth. Look.' He opened his hand, revealing Silvertooth's two silver teeth.

'The Scoffle spat them out,' Valentine said. 'Remember? This is all that's left of Sebarino Silvertooth. I thought you might like them as a memento.'

Alfie looked down at the two silver teeth and felt faint. 'No, thank you, Valentine. A memento like that might appeal to a vampire. After all, vampires have a thing about teeth, but I don't want them. I'd rather not be reminded of Silvertooth ever again.'

Valentine's face dropped. 'Oh, sorry. I've done something stupid again, of course. I guess that's why I never make any friends.'

Mum walked over to him. 'Wait a second. I'm glad you've come, Valentine. It's given me an idea. We can bury those teeth in the garden. Then we'll have done with Silvertooth for ever.'

Everyone thought it was a good idea, even Valentine. Tim's father had an old cigar box to put the silver teeth into.

'I bet he'd like that,' said Tim, 'he was always smoking those foul smelling cigars.'

Dad looked round the garden for a good

spot and ended up digging a hole next to where Tim's dead goldfish was buried. Everyone stood around the grave while Alfie carefully lowered the box into it.

'Rest in peace, Silvertooth,' said Tim's father. 'Best wishes from the bug-eyed blue-crested nincompoop. And hopefully you never come back as a vampire.'

Mum nudged him with her elbow. 'William!'

Dad smiled. 'I was just joking. If you're burying a couple of teeth, surely you're allowed to joke around.'

When everyone was back inside, Tim couldn't bear it any more. 'When are we going to finally tell Alfie? About the surprise.'

Mum and Dad looked at each other. 'You tell him, Tim.'

Alfie didn't understand at all. What was going on? It was making him nervous. Tim walked over to him and wrapped an arm around Alfie's shoulder. 'Alfie, we've adopted you.'

Alfie's mouth fell open, Valentine groaned, Noura gasped.

'What did you say?' whispered Alfie.

'We've adopted you for real,' Dad said. 'With all the documents. We should have done it a long time ago. Now no more crazy uncles can come and take you away.'

Mum nodded approvingly. 'From now on, we'll kick those crazy uncles straight out the door.' She gave Alfie a kiss.

Tears were pouring down Valentine's face. 'How beautiful,' he sniffed. 'I wish someone would adopt me. Preferably someone who works at a blood bank or in a hospital.'

The grin on Alfie's face seemed to be stuck there permanently. A lovely warm sensation flooded through his veins and wolf fur started to appear on his arms and face. His ears and nose grew, his hands and feet turned into paws.

'What's happening, Alfie? It's not even full moon!' Tim exclaimed.

'*Wrow*, I know, but I'm so happy I'm

changing anyway.'

He gave Noura a gentle lick on her nose, then ran out of the house. Everyone walked back into the garden.

'Alfie, where are you going?' called Tim.

'*Wrow!* I'm going to tell Grandpa and Leo.' The next moment he was jumping over the gate, howling with joy. Everyone felt happy and glad. Valentine raised a hand.

'Bye-bye, Alfie the Werewolf's family. I'm off.'

They waved goodbye, as he rose up into the air above the garden.

'Cool,' said Dad. 'I wish I could do that. Maybe being a vampire would be something for me.'

Valentine was already floating up above the roof.

'Drop by sometime,' called Dad.

'Gladly!' Valentine called back. 'Maybe next time you can adopt me too?'

There was no answer and when Valentine looked down he saw that the garden was suddenly deserted. They had all hurried

inside, quietly closing the door behind them.

'Hmmm,' said Valentine. 'Maybe that was asking a little too much.' He flew on, floating in front of the moon like a shadow. From somewhere in the depths below him, he heard joyful howls in the woods.

'Bye, Alfie the Werewolf,' called Valentine. 'See you later, friend.'

Turn the page for a sneak peek at
WOLF WOOD,
the next Alfie the Werewolf
adventure...

1

Werewolves

It was quiet in Wolf Wood and the full moon was looking down over the trees. The sky was already turning a slightly lighter blue. Dewdrops were glistening on the moss and the birds were about to wake up.

Suddenly there was a loud roar. *WROW!* Followed by a voice. 'Grandpa, careful, there are werewolves here.'

Grandpa shot up, his hat tumbling to the ground. 'What? Werewolves? Where? Who?'

'Here, Grandpa, us two. You and me.'

Grandpa peered at a white hairy face with a cheerful grin. A face with two pointy ears and round glasses.

'Alfie,' he smiled, baring his sharp teeth. His yellow eyes gleamed as he bent down to pick up his hat. 'Of course, you're right again. How silly of me. It's us, you and me.' He put his hat back on his black wolf's head. 'Practical joker. I suppose you thought I was asleep.'

Alfie growled and sniggered at the same time. '*Wrow*.' His white tail swished over the ground.

Grandpa Werewolf was sitting next to Alfie with his back against the trunk of an enormous tree. Grandpa rapped on the bark. 'Did you know that my tree is the oldest tree in Wolf Wood, Alfie?'

'Really?'

'Yep and it's in the exact middle of the wood. My good old tree.' Suddenly Grandpa Werewolf gave an enormous yawn. 'Oowaahh. Sorry, Alfie. How's the Scoffle?'

'Fine, Grandpa. It's still in the cage in

our garden.'

'It hasn't eaten anyone lately?'

'No, thank goodness. As long as we feed it on time, it's not dangerous. I think it's sweet.'

Grandpa Werewolf nodded. 'Good. Of course, the Scoffle is still a wild animal. It belongs in a forest, really. But maybe it feels at home with you too, seeing as you're a werewolf.' Grandpa blinked and looked up at the last rays of moonlight. 'Oops,' he exclaimed.

2

Voices

'What is it, Grandpa?' Startled, Alfie looked at Grandpa Werewolf, who was pointing at the moon with his walking stick.

'You have to go home, Alfie, it's got very late. Or rather, it's become very early, almost morning. We've been sitting here far too long. Time always flies when you're having fun. The sun will come up soon and in a little while you'll turn back into a boy again.'

Alfie nodded. 'In a few hours I have to go to school, that's the worst part. I've been up all night. Hopefully I won't fall asleep at school. That's already happened a couple of times. The teacher kept me in.' He opened his jaws wide and yawned. 'I'm exhausted.'

Grandpa Werewolf struggled to his feet. 'It's a shame. I was just about to tell you the big secret.'

'You were going to tell me a secret?'

'Yes, the secret of Werewolf Wood. But it's too late for that now.'

'A big secret? What big secret?'

Grandpa Werewolf shook his head. 'No, Alfie, not now. You have to take your time for a big secret. You have to sit down and relax. The two of us, you and me, werewolves together. And then you have to tell it at your leisure.' He winked. 'Next time.'

'Ohhh.' Alfie was burning with curiosity. 'Can't you just tell me a little bit now?'

'No, you have to race off home.' Grandpa's yellow eyes gleamed. 'I think I'll climb up into my wolf's nest and hit the sack.'

Alfie looked up at the rope ladder hanging down from the tree. Hidden carefully between the leaves and the branches was a fantastic treehouse.

Wolf Wood was actually a Werewolf Wood, but that was something only werewolves knew. Grandpa was a werewolf the whole time, both day and night. He was able to do that because he was already very old.

Alfie only changed at full moon when, for three nights in a row, he would turn into a small white werewolf with glasses on his snout. As soon as the sun came up, he changed back into an ordinary little boy.

Grandpa Werewolf patted Alfie briefly on the head, then grabbed the rope ladder. 'See you soon, Alfie. Run off home now.' Quickly, he climbed up the ladder.

Grandpa's amazing, thought Alfie. He's as agile as a young monkey.

When he'd made it to the top, Grandpa Werewolf looked down grinning. 'Don't dawdle anywhere, Alfie. Morning's coming. I'll tell you the secret next time.'

'Goodnight, Grandpa.'

Grandpa winked at Alfie, pulled up

the rope ladder and disappeared behind the branches.

'*Wrow*, time to race home.' Alfie dropped down on to all fours and tore through the forest. Soon it would be light. He thought about what Grandpa Werewolf had said. The secret of Werewolf Wood . . . What could it be?

Suddenly he froze. His ears quivered. He stuck his nose up into the air and sniffed.

Branches snapped. Leaves rustled.

Alfie sniffed again. The wind was carrying strange smells towards him. Unknown smells. Trouble.

'Owahhh.' Alfie couldn't suppress a yawn. He clapped a paw over his mouth in fright. What was that over there? A beam of light between the trees. Was that a torch? A patch of light danced over the trunks. Then he heard strange voices. People! What were they doing in the wood this early? Had they heard him? Alfie dived behind a bush and kept as quiet as a mouse. He yawned again, but silently this time.

The people came closer. Now their deep voices were loud and clear.

'Can you picture it, Rattlebones? Beautiful blocks of flats, the smell of asphalt. Smell it? Lovely! Plenty of parking. At most a couple of football pitches, otherwise no green. Bah.'

'That's right, Boss. Get rid of those sloppy trees. Flatten the lot. We'll make it nice and flat for some nice new flats.'

'Exactly. Very wise, Rattlebones. If you want to build, you have to flatten something first.'

'Absolutely, Boss. And we'll sell the wood for a tidy little profit on the side.'

Alfie didn't get it. What were they talking about? A flat wood?

Suddenly a light swept over his face, catching him full in the eyes and momentarily blinding him. He dived deeper into the undergrowth.

To be continued in

Wolf Wood

Another

ALFIE THE WEREWOLF

adventure

Birthday Surprise

Alfie is no ordinary boy –
at full moon he transforms
into a werewolf!

It's Alfie's birthday and he's turning more
than just a year older. Something strange is
happening to him. First comes fur ...
then claws ... and then a TAIL. Before he
knows it, Alfie's a furry white werewolf!

He's going to have to get used to his new
wolfish lifestyle, and stay away from next
door's chickens ... who knew turning
seven would be this scary?

Another

ALFIE THE WEREWOLF

adventure

Full Moon

Alfie is no ordinary boy –
at full moon he transforms
into a werewolf!

Alfie is on a school trip for two nights
of campfires, ghost stories and a spooky
outing into eerie Sulphur Forest.
The children aren't scared, but perhaps
they should be – something strange
is lurking amongst the trees, and what's
more ... there's a full moon
and Alfie's on the loose!